THE SATYR

Robert DeMaria

THE SATYR

 SECOND CHANCE PRESS
Noyac Road
Sag Harbor, NY 11963

originally published by W.H. Allen & Co. Ltd., London in 1972
and in the United States by Bobbs-Merrill

Copyright © 1972 by Robert DeMaria
All rights reserved, including the right to reproduce
this book, or parts thereof, in any form, except
for the inclusion of brief quotes in a review.

Library of Congress Cataloging-in-Publication Data

DeMaria, Robert.
    The satyr / by Robert DeMaria
       p.   cm.
    ISBN 0-933256-78-7 : $21.95
    I. Title.
    PS3554.E455S28   1992
813' .54--dc20   91-39571
                                            CIP

Manufactured in the United States of America

SECOND CHANCE PRESS
Noyac Road
Sag Harbor, NY 11963

"What should such fellows as I do
crawling between heaven and earth?"

Hamlet, Act III, Scene 1

Sunday, 11 May

I decided today that I would kill my mother, and I feel I ought to explain why.

I am a very unusual person. I am, for one thing, a kind of literary genius. I dream metaphors. I know the secret meanings of words. I understand the magic of poetry. I feel, at times, that I can open my mouth and allow to issue therefrom a stream of verbal music. I am also a highly sensitive and intelligent person. I see things instantly as they are. I have a painfully sharp sense of reality—and, of course, of the absurdity of that reality. I am not fooled by any philosophy or religion. I know that any moment now I am going to die and that that death will be absolute.

In this journal I will be honest. I will put down the events of each day exactly as they occur. I am not afraid of guilt or incrimination. I see myself already as the ghost of myself, performing for some as yet unborn audience in some unimaginable age in the future. (Could Shakespeare have imagined a New York production of *Hamlet*?) The pity of it is that, as long as we are alive, we have to do these honest things in the dark. If the world knew any of us as we really are, it would instantly kill us.

My name is Marc McMann. I am thirty-five years old (time slips away like eels). I live beyond my means in an apartment on East Eleventh Street in the Village, a few blocks from the Ransom-McKenzie Publishing Company, where I am an editor in the English division of the College Text Department. I play midwife to ambitious but starving little academicians, who are convinced that they can achieve instant success and write their rotten philosophical novels by publishing dreary handbooks and anthologies for Freshman English courses. It is embarrassing for them and amusing for me that they should write so badly. I correct their mistakes and take them to lunch, where invariably they get drunk on the one martini that they can not afford not to order since the lunch is free. They tell me all about their fantastically boring PhD dissertations and their secret literary ambitions, which usually consist of an unfinished Joycean piece of fiction, so riddled with erudition that it will shatter the minds of the three or four people in the universe capable of reading it should it ever achieve publication. I hate my job. And I hate the authors of the garbage I am forced to process. But until I achieve the recognition that I deserve, or until my mother dies and passes on to me the small fortune that is rightfully mine, I have no choice but to spend myself in this depressing way. I have been with Ransom-McKenzie since I graduated from Columbia College, where I majored in English, but my rise in the company has been un-meteoric, to say the least, because of certain 'personality difficulties,' and because of certain little Jewish intellectuals who have bargained and ass-kissed their way into jobs I might have had, were I less true to myself.

There is not much to tell about my way of life. I like Camus, professional football, and masturbation. We are told that masturbation is a somewhat excusable habit that comes upon pubescent boys and is traded in eventually for healthier and more patriotic sexual activities, but I have never given it up. And time and experience have helped me to master the art. I may one day write a book on the subject—a very poetic book. Of all the sexual activities it is the simplest. It requires no courtship or seduction, no sophomoric preliminary conversations about Senator McCarthy or Timothy Leary. One simply grabs hold of oneself, without the anxiety of possible rejection, and, with a little imagination, commits whatever criminal act one pleases.

Though I dwell on the delights of this delicious pastime, I am not uninterested in other forms of sexual recreation, all the way from the little rituals of the suburbs to the Outer Mongolia of the bizarre. My impulses have been the subject of considerable discussion with my analyst, Dr. Popoff, who speaks to me in textbooks about passions he has never understood.

I am a bachelor and may remain one as long as my mother is alive, though I am engaged to a beautiful girl named Laura Haley, who is scheduled to surrender her virgin self to me for life in about three weeks, at an Episcopal church in Garden City. It is my impending marriage, in fact, that has brought the entire situation to a head. My mother, you see, objects vigorously. And when my mother objects vigorously to anything, it is like a nameless and invisible plague being visited upon the land. You know it is killing you, but you can't describe exactly how it is being done.

My mother's name is Gertrude McMann. My father's name was Eli. We have a house in Lloyd Harbor, Long Island, where I grew up in deadly cycles of winter, spring, summer, and fall, protected from the pollution of friends and the hazards of toys.

My mother is so utterly secretive about everything that I know next to nothing about my early years, except that my father was a wealthy industrialist with a factory in Queens, which produced something during World War II that was essential for killing foreigners. He was twenty years older than my mother and appears in an old photograph behind a huge moustache with a wet and lecherous lower lip. Since he died when I was only three, I never really knew him. He survives as a rotund shadow and a blast of bad breath that may have been a blend of cigar smoke and whisky. Since my mother is evasive, I have had to conjure up a father who probably never existed. In my mind he is presidential in the old manner, like Grover Cleveland or Teddy Roosevelt. He sits immobile in a great armchair, his thumbs tucked into the pockets of his vest, which are linked by a giant watch-chain. He seems stuffed, the masterwork of some anonymous taxidermist. His eyes stare glassily at mahogany panelling and shelves of leather-bound books with uncut pages. The hunter who bagged this remarkable specimen was, of course, my mother, her gun still smoking years later.

If I seem to be suggesting that my mother killed my father, it is only because I can not imagine any man surviving even one day in the same house with her, let alone four years. And, what's more, the circumstances of his death are mysterious. My mother and father set sail for Bloc Island in their thirty-eight-foot sloop, *The Albatross*. Two days later she returned alone with the unlikely story that he had fallen overboard in the night and disappeared. It is quite possible, of course, that the wretched man, finding himself in such intimate quarters with Gertrude, chose to commit suicide but it is not likely that such an expert swimmer and sailor, as he was, would drown accidentally in the middle of a calm summer night. His body was never recovered. Is it possible that she ate him?

From the very beginning my relationship with my mother was a disaster. And by the *beginning* I mean not only my birth, but a terrible period just prior to it. It all came back to me one day, as though in a vision, an act of total recall. It is generally assumed that the foetus does not want to be born, that the spasms that drive it from the womb are like the hands of the invisible executioner in this life. But I found this was not so in my case.

I was cuddled there, all wet and wrinkled, an old man in that short span of life, the ultimate stage in the evolutionary drama that we all rehearse from conception to birth. I was very warm in the darkness, and in a kind of trance or sleep until the signs of danger woke me. I was immersed in an endless dream of life. I even dimly remember my earlier, sub-human forms. It was all continuous. Life flowed together from the first cell to the most complex beast. And all was surrounded by darkness. And all pulsed and throbbed as though we were in a giant drum. I was sperm and germ. I was tadpole and lizard and fish. I was amphibious and simian. I was Man, that paragon of animals. And my world was the small dark universe that I could feel on all sides. It touched me and I knew it was there. It fed me. It gave me life. I did not know what was beyond it. I clung instinctively to the body that was trying to create me as a separate creature. At least until that terrifying moment, when I first sensed that my mother was trying to kill me.

If you have seen the animal terror in the flushed bird or the hooked fish or the stampeded herd, then you know what I felt. A warning came through the blood and I knew in an instant that my mother was not going to allow me to be born. She was going to suffocate me and then ingest me again into her body or into her human sewerage system and, thus, be rid of me. I could feel her trying. I could feel the opening close. She was in general rebellion against the very idea of childbirth, a fact confirmed later on by the need for an emergency caesarian. But they cut her open and out I came, gasping for air, as though I had been underwater a long time.

I cursed her with my first desperate breath, in language she would have understood had she not been drugged. But I was to repeat my message a thousand times over. There never was a child who cried so persistently and loudly and who chomped so viciously at the nipples of milkless bags. I wanted to eat her. I wanted to destroy her utterly. She betrayed me. Not only in the womb, but in her arms and at her breast. Surrounded by doctors and nurses, she shivered and cried and complained. She fell into a fit of depression and refused to see me for two weeks. I was given a loveless bottle by a fat nurse with an enormous bosom. My infantile thoughts were already lecherous. I felt those mounds of flesh. I knew they were not my mother's. And yet I enjoyed them. Already, I was a criminal.

In all fairness, though, I must say on Gertrude's behalf that I was an ugly and disgusting child. Not only did I cry endlessly and mercilessly but I was fond of vomiting and my digestive system might have been a straight tube with an irreparable leak. My diapers were always filthy and from my belly to my thighs I was all red raw meat and scabs. I was bald and cross-eyed and never smiled. I had the wrinkles and the expression of an eighty-year-old, a kind of premature King Lear, who has felt the lashes and lightning of nature's cruelty.

Since Gertrude had muffed her chance to kill me and since I was as yet too small to kill her, we had to arrive at some sort of a working agreement. Her terms, though, were difficult. She would provide me with all the things I needed to survive and to grow up, as long as I obeyed her absolutely and did not in any way interfere with her real life, which was a kind of perfumed secret that I always associated with a locked bureau drawer and a rubber bag high on a hook in the bathroom. My glimpses into her private life were always surreptitious, of course. I would sneak into her room when she was busy elsewhere. I would go into her closet and touch her empty dresses. And I would lie on her bed with a delicious criminal feeling.

My favourite form of indecent pleasure in those early years was to watch my mother bathe. To accomplish this precocious act of voyeurism I had to do desperate and ingenious things. Once I hid in the wicker hamper and peered at her through the weave. She never discovered me, but she dropped on my head a pair of stinking silk underwear. At other times, I had to be satisfied with the limited view provided by the keyhole, but that was eventually stuffed with cotton. My long-range plan was to bore a hole through my bedroom wall, which I could conceal on my side under the picture of Little Boy Blue. However, not having heard as yet of the two-way mirror, I never found the crucial half of the solution.

Until I went to school, I had no friends at all. We had sufficient acreage to keep us out of contact with our neighbours and my mother was not an overly friendly sort. When I inquired about the larger world, when I asked who lived here or there, pointing sometimes to the Parsons' house or to the Grants', a pained expression would come over her face, as though someone were slowly inserting a needle in her heart. 'They're not the sort of people we're interested in,' she would say. 'And their children are absolute monsters.' Taking her literally, I would sometimes crawl through the underbrush Indian fashion to spy on these 'monsters'. But all I ever saw in the Parsons' yard were two boys a bit older than me, delightfully filthy, laughing amidst mud castles and home-made scooters. The Grants had three little girls, whose shrieks and giggles I could only assume were the mystery language of demons and witches. I tried to persuade myself that I was lucky to be so well-guarded in our elegant house, safe from the wrong kind of people and those monsters disguised as ordinary children.

It seems to me that I spent much of my time being bathed and brushed and combed. My mother was especially concerned about my teeth and would, several times a day, ram a toothbrush into my mouth in order to destroy by brute force any presumptuous germ that dared to appear there. I dreaded her assault on my tender mouth, but after a while, I knew that any complaint on my part would be met by a hysterical lecture on that invisible world of voracious creatures who were trying to devour my precious little body.

My mother never kissed me, but sometimes, especially at night, before I outgrew the tucking-in ritual, she would lean over me and kiss the air an inch or so from my cheek. O lucky air! But I was not destined to go unkissed forever. When I was about six, we took on a new maid, a plump, dumb woman about thirty years old, unmarried, childless and quite homely, except for her glow of bovine good health. Her name was Clara and she spoke with an accent. We soon became lovers. And after the lights were out in my room and I was efficiently filed away for the night, she would tip-toe in, her finger at her lips. I caught the conspiratorial air immediately and knew exactly what to do. At first she would only sit on my bed and quietly sing to me and then bid me good night with a rough squeeze and a warm kiss. But after a while, she took to pressing me for longer and longer periods to her abundant bosom and feeling my limbs and body as though she were examining me for defects. I was delighted. Gertrude had given me the impression that human contact was sinful and I was starved for the feel of living flesh. If there was one thing Clara had an abundance of, it was flesh.

I don't remember exactly when Clara first bared her giant bosom to me, but what a heavenly revelation. She started appearing in my room wearing only an old woollen robe. It was a simple matter for her to let it fall open as we cuddled and courted. She pressed my face against her hot breasts. I could feel her breathing. Her hands wandered over my back and into my pyjamas. They caressed my buttocks and thighs—and eventually my pathetically little genitals. This all happened by degrees, though in my mind time has collapsed and it all runs together as a gorgeous period of infantile debauchery. Eventually, my mouth, as though it had a brain of its own, discovered those knobs that were her nipples and knew what to do with them. I pushed my face into the sea of flesh. I suckled and nuzzled and slipped each night into a euphoric sleep, into a child's dreamworld in which everything was made of candy and cake.

13

Time passed and I grew to be a sturdy lad but our evening ritual continued. Sometimes Clara would lie down beside me, her bulk tipping the mattress in her direction, so that I would roll downhill towards her. We would snuggle under the covers and she would deftly remove my pyjamas and open her robe. She was a whole landscape of flesh, with rolling hills and valleys, mounds and gorges. Once she took my hand and lost it in the black forest of her crotch. I didn't quite understand, but it made her sigh, so I didn't mind. When she pressed it further I could feel a great damp swamp and all I could think was that she had another mouth down there. It took a while for my factual knowledge to catch up with my carnal knowledge. Inarticulate Clara was not very helpful.

Like a hot-house plant under twenty-four hours of artificial light and nourished by fertilisers, I developed at a remarkable rate. Clara's efforts were rewarded by precocious growth and by the first inklings of a real orgasm at the age of ten. When I described the wonderful new sensation to her, she smiled broadly and said, 'Now you are a man.' Whereupon she hauled me on top of her and guided me roughly into that invisible swamp. Nature took hold from that point on, but nothing much happened. I was like a minnow lost at sea. The posture, however, was nice. I was still short enough to lie on her breasts like pillows and take the button of her nipple in my mouth. I was connected at both ends, which seemed to me a natural and desirable state of affairs. I wasn't really sure what the point of it all was, but I wasn't about to ruin a good thing by asking too many questions.

That we should get caught eventually, I suppose, was inevitable. We got over-confident. We did not always wait until Gertrude was safely in bed or out of the house. Clara, in her mid-thirties, was at the height of her sexual desperation. She did not always restrain her heaving moans of satisfaction. And under the strain of her enormous bulk my poor little bed threatened to collapse. When it finally did one night, Gertrude appeared with such suddenness that there was no time to feign innocence. We were both stark naked and I was sitting astride poor startled Clara, as though I expected her to gallop off into the land of cowboys and Indians. Gertrude reeled and started to faint.

Her mouth moved furiously for thirty seconds before the first trembling words came out. Fortunately for me, she levelled her attack mainly at Clara. She called her a monstrous whore, a beast, a maniac, a slut, a seducer of children, and a dozen or so other things that I can no longer remember. Needless to say, I never saw Clara again, my first, and, in many ways, my favourite mistress.

Though I did not fully comprehend the nature of my crime, I knew that I had come close to destroying Gertrude by my involvement with Clara. Her horror and confusion were mixed, I am sure, with a kind of jealousy. She was unable to speak to me for a week. Though she despised cooking and she herself had lost her appetite, she prepared for me the most elaborate meals. We would sit alone in the large dining room, the dozen candles of the candelabra flickering nervously. I didn't dare speak for fear of saying the wrong thing. And she seemed incapable of forcing into words the nightmarish ideas that seemed to be running through her tortured mind. I nibbled dutifully at the feast that she had spread before me, until I felt I had consumed enough to satisfy her. And then I waited, as if for the end of the world, until she stopped staring at me and got up to clear away the dishes. In our new language, I knew that this was my signal to retreat to my room, where I listened like a spy to a barely audible radio, that brought me personal messages from the outside world in the form of 'The Lone Ranger' and 'The Green Hornet'.

In that terrible week Gertrude grew thin and pale. It was summertime and I did not even have the refuge of school. Her worn face and tragic eyes revealed some of the questions that plagued her. Was I an unnatural child? Would I grow up to be a sex maniac or a rapist? Was I, in fact, already one? Did I do this awful thing just to wound her? And what awful things would I do next? How had she failed me? Hadn't she done everything for me that a mother could possibly do? And then the most important question, accompanied by her grimmest stare: Was she safe in the same house with me?

When she finally collected herself sufficiently to speak, she approached me with the formality and trepidation of an ambassador on his first visit to a nation of headhunters. 'I feel there is something we must discuss,' she said, her voice full of official credentials. Her subject was sex, of course, and her principal conclusion was that I was to have nothing to do with it. 'The time will come,' she said, 'when you will have strange urges. When you do, I hope you will come to me.' She blushed. 'I mean, perhaps I can help you.' In what way, I wondered, but kept my eyes averted and said nothing. Then she began to speak very rapidly about how unfortunate it was that my father was not here to explain these things to me and about how she had to be both father and mother to me. She paused and fiddled with her beads. If I *were*, indeed, the leader of a head-hunting tribe, I would have at that moment nodded my black decorated face towards my Secretary of State, who would have lopped off her silly head with a flick of his machete. 'There is nothing basically wrong with sex,' she went on, 'but it is an activity reserved for adults, especially married adults. It is nature's way of reproducing the race and ought not to be abused.' She explained how the abuse of sex often led to crime, madness, disease, and moral decay. 'You must resist the temptations and turn your mind to more constructive things.'

I was very solemn during this whole interview. And when she was through I nodded to indicate that I understood. She dabbed at the dampness of her forehead with her handkerchief, smiled bravely at me, as though from her deathbed, and retreated. Though I thought most of what she said was idiotic, my murderous heart must have been touched in some way, because I decided to make an effort to be good. For my mother's sake, I promised myself that I would keep my filthy little hands off my filthy little tool and forget about Clara's engulfing boobs. I would take up something 'constructive', as Gertrude put it, something that would improve my life and make me a worthy human being. I decided that it would not be airplane models, because I did not like the way the glue stuck to my fingers. A tree-house seemed too imposing a task, especially for one who was basically inept at such things. I considered writing, but soon discovered that I had nothing to say. Finally, I settled on art. I would be an artist. I would draw and paint. It was the perfect thing. It would keep my hands above the table, and it would please Gertrude, who was always talking to me about culture, which I vaguely associated with French horns and seascapes.

I worked furiously for about a week. I drew trees and ships and houses. I became absorbed and excited. I graduated to people. I drew them in every conceivable context. But then something began to happen. My people got uglier and uglier. They became monstrous. I armed them with guns and swords. I threw them in the fire. I bombed them with Stukas. I cut off their arms and legs and took off all their clothes. I wore out my red crayon with blood and gore. And then I became obsessed with genitals and breasts. I made dragons with giant erections out of which fire spouted. I made women with hair to the ground and breasts to match and then ran them over with Panzer tanks. My masterpiece was a woman with balloons for breasts, who was being strangled by a phallic snake. Out of her massive black bush there emerged a tiny creature with bulging eyes, from which blood dripped like tears. I finished the picture in a fever of effort and was immediately seized with a fit of panic. I knew in that instant that the emerging creature was somehow me.

Trembling all over, I gathered together every drawing or painting I had made that week and stuffed them under my mattress. Then I locked myself in the bathroom and did not emerge until my pubescent digit was severely and dangerously abused.

This violent episode really launched my career as a masturbator. Until the great scandal, I could rely on Clara. Afterwards, I was driven by a terrible desperation. I had to reassure myself constantly. Over and over again I would achieve that tickle of my diminutive orgasm. Five, six, ten times a day. I learned all the tricks. I tore holes in the pockets of my pants. I embraced my pillow. Foam rubber drove me wild. I took half a dozen showers a day. I used every conceivable form of lubrication. And to escape detection I became as skilful as a secret agent. I knew that Gertrude was watching me. We were an odd pair in that big house. She hid everything from me and I hid everything from her. We didn't trust each other. We were afraid of each other.

Dr. Popoff and I have discussed this mysterious 'fear'. His notion is the orthodox one, that poor Gertrude, brought up to

17

despise men, castrated them in a thousand subtle and unconscious ways. 'But she is only being defensive,' he said. 'She is really just a frightened little girl who needs help.' What kind of help, I wondered. And then I had a vision of myself in black tights and Renaissance tunic. I was princely and girlish with Botticelli hair. There was no bulge in my crotch, only a little V. I was approaching Gertrude, who sat on a throne. I held out a green velvet pillow with gold tassels at the corners. On the pillow was a jewelled box. And in the box, my gift to Gertrude, was my amputated little worm. I knelt before her. She bowed from the neck and smiled royally. When she opened the box, a little squeal of delight escaped from her lips. She picked up the shrivelled symbol of my manhood in her ringed fingers (there was a ring on every finger, including the thumb), and, in two or three bites, ate it like a country sausage.

What Popoff fails to understand is that Gertrude doesn't only want to castrate me; she wants to kill me. I have tried frequently to explain this to him, but he only gives me a fatherly smile, as if to say, 'Don't be paranoiac. Nobody ever really kills anybody.' I take a deep breath and try again, at forty dollars an hour, but my language is too poetic. 'It's my soul she wants.' Dr. Popoff doesn't understand 'soul'. He looks at me more closely, as if perhaps I am a madman after all. And then suddenly, the time is up and he flicks open the venetian blinds to let in a flood of sunlight.

His final nickel's worth of advice as he ushers me out of his office is that 'the fear is irrational'. But, damn it, Gertrude is a dangerous woman. All my life she has kept me at her mercy. She has threatened me with disapproval, loss of affection, anger, guilt, and disinheritance. She has convinced me that her happiness depends entirely on me. She keeps trying to drive the spike of guilt into my heart. I have come to the point where I can not obey her or ignore her, where I can not keep her happy and don't dare make her unhappy. Only her death will resolve things, and, since she is not likely to die for another twenty or thirty years, I have no choice but to kill her.

The thing above all others that I despised about her in my earlier years was the way she tried to make me her little 'husband'. I was expected to escort her everywhere. Keep in mind that my mother is barely twenty years older than me, and that she is one of those neat, compact women who always look considerably younger than they are, especially as they approach middle age. Her features are delicate and well defined. Her eyes are very blue and her lips are almost too thin. Her figure is a divine masterpiece of economy and efficiency. Not a bone is larger than it ought to be. Her breasts are aesthetically adequate, and her flesh is firm. She has boasted that she has weighed 110 pounds since she graduated from grammar school. When she was twenty-five, she looked like a teenager, and when she was forty she might easily have passed for ten years younger. She would take me to charity dinners, weddings and gallery openings and exhibit me to evoke compliments about her youthful appearance. I was the perfect foil. I had emerged from the ugliness of my early years into a tall, sturdy lad, combining the muscularity of my father and the handsomeness of my mother, to whom I bear an unusual and depressing facial resemblance. I can not look at myself in the mirror without seeing her. I sometimes wish that I had a scar or that kind of rough masculine face that excites women. But no, I've got this neat handsomeness, this boyishness. I am Jack Armstrong, the All-American Boy, the winner of the 220-yard low hurdles, the class valedictorian.

My career as my mother's little gentleman reached ridiculous heights when I was about fifteen and she insisted that I accompany her to a New Year's Eve masquerade party at the lavish home of Dr. Molinar, the director of The North Shore Medical Center. I hated parties but I loved disguises and masquerades. (Perhaps I should have been an actor.) The possibilities raced through my mind like characters in a wax museum. I would be Captain Hook, the Hunchback of Notre Dame, the Man in the Iron Mask. I was mentally painting on moustaches and shoving daggers in my belt when Gertrude said something, as though from another room, about Romeo and Juliet. The idea was to me so inconceivable that it made me dizzy.

I refused, of course, in the strongest language I dared to use. She pleaded. I went into the kitchen and had a glass of milk and a piece of cake. She followed me. I said the whole idea was ridiculous. She said Dr. Molinar was fond of Shakespeare. I said that in that case I would go as Caliban. She didn't recognise the reference. She said she had once played Juliet in a school production and that, besides, Romeo was a teenager. 'No,' I shouted, spouting cake crumbs in her direction. She switched to outrage and said that I should not speak to her in that tone of voice. I wanted to say she was lucky that I didn't bury a dagger in her throat but instead I went to my room and closed the door. About half an hour later, she came in timidly, her eyes red and a martyr's smile on her pale face. Lowering my copy of *Crime and Punishment*, I watched her approach. She sat down on the edge of the bed and fiddled with her beads, as though she were saying her rosary. In the midst of my rage, I must confess that I was struck by her beauty. Had she planned it that way, I wonder? Did she rub her eyes on purpose? Did she inhale onion fumes? What a saintly pose of gorgeous agony and sacrifice! My adolescent heart was moved. 'Never mind,' she said. 'We'll stay home instead, just the two of us, and have a quiet New Year's Eve.' Needless to say, her evil strategy destroyed my defences utterly and I agreed to go.

But the moment Gertrude produced the costumes I regretted my weakness. They were the usual Romeo and Juliet stage outfits, rented from some theatrical costumier. It was Romeo's black tights that filled me with panic. For Christ's sake, I thought, I might as well be naked. Every curve, bulge and crack will be on display. I thought of faggy ballet dancers with their revealed asses. 'Why is the jacket so short?' I said. Because the costumes were authentic, she explained.

In the week that preceded the great event, I tried on my tights a thousand times, but I could find no adequate way to protect my exposed rear or to cover the embarrassing bulge that announced my gender. At last I was struck with a minor inspiration: though I could not play it, I would carry my guitar. Gertrude put up a mild objection on the grounds of anachronism but I was adamant.

At the party, I kept trying to sit down, but my mother kept introducing me to people and I was forced to perform my little act as her son-escort-husband-lover. But between me and that world of phoney musketeers and Cinderellas I kept my musical cod-piece, my unstrummed guitar.

Eventually, I was able to retreat into a corner, where I stood, traumatised and trembling, behind a spidery metal lamp. Gertrude was wafted into the alcoholic guts of the party. She drank champagne and danced and giggled politely at the whispered inanities of dandified doctors and lascivious lawyers.

Time passed slowly, inching its way towards midnight and the new year. The tension mounted. The masquerading middle class collected itself for its annual ritual, its spasm of nostalgia, self-pity, and lust. The countdown was provided by a television set. There was a hush, a pause. And finally the magic moment and the hollow outburst. There was a lot of kissing and shouting and some feeble horn-blowing. And then it all subsided again into tinkling ice-cubes, music and shifting arrangements of fairy-land characters. Peter Rabbit fondled Moll Flanders. Tarzan discussed politics with Humpty Dumpty. And Snow White danced with Jack the Ripper.

By 2 a.m., the crowd began to thin out. But the hard-core drinkers and the long-distance talkers remained. Gertrude was surrounded by three men who were urging her to recite some lines from *Romeo and Juliet*. 'No, no, no,' she said, meaning, 'of course I will, if properly pursued.' Her lurching promoters were Dracula, Wolf-Man, and Frankenstein's monster. They dragged her to the centre of the living room and called for silence.

In his Transylvanian accent, Dracula said, 'Our little Sweetheart of Forest Lawn has consented to give us a scene from "The Tragedy of Romeo and Juliet".' Applause. He smiled at her with his thin, lip-sticked mouth and bounced his black eyebrows. Sweeping his cape around her he said, 'And what shall it be, my dear?'

'Well,' she said, eyelids fluttering and body floating on champagne. 'In honour of you kind gentlemen, how about the death scene?' Applause and shouts of encouragement.

'But where's the corpse?' said Wolf-Man. 'Where's Romeo?' Mumbling and searching. A shriek of terror from the corner with the spidery lamp.

Stiff-legged, flat-headed, and drunk, Frankenstein's monster approached me in my hiding place. He toppled a chair, growled and grunted, brushed away imaginary cobwebs and took hold of me so roughly that my guitar was torn away and clattered to the floor. He lifted me bodily, and I was too shocked to resist. He delivered me to Gertrude, laying me out on the rug, arranging me for the big scene. 'You're dead,' he said, 'and don't forget it.' Gertrude asked for a cup and placed it beside the 'body'.

She explained the scene. 'Romeo has killed Paris in a fight and then poisons himself because he thinks Juliet is dead. They are in the vault in the churchyard. Juliet is just waking from her death-like sleep. 'The Lady stirs,' says Friar Laurence. Gertrude circled the 'stage' once, twice, and descended to the rug, where I, para-lysed by fear, was on the brink of becoming a real corpse. She lay down beside me. I didn't dare look at her, but I could smell her. My eyes were closed and I imagined that the bulge in my tights was a veritable volcano, that might at any moment erupt un-controllably and wipe out the entire community.

Juliet stirred and then sat up. 'The Friar leaves,' she whispered. She looked around and discovered her dead lover. She gasped. She cried out. Shades of the silent films.

> 'What's here? A cup, closed in my true love's hand?
> Poison, I see, hath been his timeless end :
> O churl ! drunk all, and left no friendly drop
> To help me after? I will kiss thy lips;
> Haply some poison yet doth hang on them,
> To make me die with a restorative.'

She leaned over me and kissed me passionately, sucking at my mouth and sighing. 'Thy lips are warm.' Then she pulled away suddenly, as though she heard someone coming. 'Yea, noise? then I'll be brief. O happy dagger !' She took my imaginary dag-ger lovingly into her small hands. 'This is thy sheath,' she said, stabbing herself in what must have been her womb. 'There rust and let me die.' She fell across me, a dead weight on my chest. Cheers and applause !

Her monstrous promoters lifted her to her feet and kissed her. Free at last, and flushed with embarrassment, I ran out of the room and out of the house where the icy night was a friendly embrace and a dark protection from the nightmare inside.

So much for the past. I promise you I shall not be Proustian about it. I shall leap now into the present 'as swift as on the wings of meditation', and tell my story as it unfolds.

I was lying in bed this morning in a delicious half-sleep when Gertrude called to remind me that it was Mother's Day and that she expected me about noon. When the phone rang, I was lying there clutching one of those marvellous early morning erections that are created by erotic dreams and a mild pressure on the bladder, a kind of Wilkinson sabre that might be used to cut down Turks at Balaclava or raise goose-flesh on the thighs of young virgins. When Gertrude's voice chirped electronically in my ear, the proud beast in my hand shrivelled and died.

Gertrude has invented a number of private traditions that she expects me to uphold. One of them is that we have Mother's Day dinner together and that she prepares for me alone a feast fit for kings. It is her annual act of contrition among the pots and pans. I sometimes think it is her way of trying to apologise, but it never comes out quite right. Ever since I went off to College, Gertrude has had an apartment in the city overlooking Central Park. But one cannot normally expect to find her in the kitchen of that apartment except on Mother's Day. On that day, Emma, the coloured maid, goes home to her own mother and Gertrude dons her apron and tries to make up for thirty-five years of maternal failure.

I found her in the kitchen when I arrived. She looked up with an odd smile on her tight mouth and a lock of hair falling over her forehead. Her face glistened with odourless perspiration. She was St. Gertrude the martyr. The kindling was heaped about her feet. She had been denied a crucifix. But in her heart she knew that the living God loved her, though the world chose to destroy her earthly body right there in her own apartment. The whole thing was quite theatrical. It made me think that perhaps she would have succeeded as an actress after all.

In Act I, we see Gertrude, the martyred mother, looking up from the stove. The sweat leaks from her like tears, as though her entire body were weeping. I hesitate to remind her that neither the window nor the vent in the kitchen is open. I do not want to shatter the delicate china of her mood. It is sweet, really sweet. Her smile is not unlovable. Act II: In a trice, Gertrude transforms herself into the elegant hostess, talks about recent openings on Broadway, sits queen-like at the head of the overly large table and makes me feel for an hour or so like a very important court attendant. Act III: Coffee and brandy is accompanied by a motherly lecture on how I am squandering my energies and ruining my life. The little queen is now the old maid school marm and I am about to have my knuckles rapped. Her blue eyes fade a bit and grow colder. I can feel the royal report card forming in her mind.

GERTRUDE: Marc, you must begin to take your life more seriously.

MARC: Mother, I take my life very seriously—too seriously perhaps.

GERTRUDE: You are thirty-five years old. You are mature. Before long, you will be middle-aged.

MARC: Never! I am an incurable advanced adolescent.

GERTRUDE: Please don't try to be funny, Marc; it doesn't suit the occasion.

MARC: What's the occasion?

GERTRUDE: (*ignoring his question*) Have you seen Laura lately?

MARC: You know I have. Why do you ask?

GERTRUDE: In the first place I don't know that you have seen her. You never mention her. In fact, you never mention anything you do. Perhaps I ought to hire a private detective just to find out what my son is doing. Why are you so secretive? What in the world can you have to hide? You're not in any sort of trouble are you?

MARC: What would you say if I told you I was pregnant?

GERTRUDE: (*annoyed*) Don't make fun of me, Marc. Don't add cruelty to all the rest. I'm only trying to help you.

MARC: (*exasperated*) Mother, I'm not in any trouble and I'm not hiding anything from you. I never mention Laura because I know you don't like her.

GERTRUDE : I have nothing against the girl personally, mind you; I just think that it would be a disaster for you to marry her. You're not compatible in any way as far as I can see.

MARC : Well, it's a gamble I'm willing to take.

GERTRUDE : What in the world do you see in her?

MARC : She's a nice, ordinary, pretty girl.

GERTRUDE : And what makes you think a nice, ordinary, pretty girl is going to make you happy?

MARC : Would you prefer that I marry an awful, extraordinary, ugly girl?

GERTRUDE : (*thinking*) If she had the right qualities, yes! Prettiness is not everything.

MARC : Well, I'll be damned if I'm going to live in the same house for forty years with an ugly woman.

GERTRUDE : You'll soon discover that intelligence and social grace are much more important.

MARC : Intelligence is a male characteristic; it doesn't become women. And as far as the social thing is concerned—well, she comes from Garden City, for Christ's sake, what more do you want?

GERTRUDE : Garden City is not what it used to be. And, besides, her family lives in a development house.

MARC : Mother, you amaze me. You take up all kinds of liberal causes but you're an old-fashioned snob.

GERTRUDE : (*angry*) Don't be ridiculous. I'm only trying to help you find a suitable wife.

MARC : I've found one.

GERTRUDE : She's fourteen years younger than you. She's virtually uneducated. It took her nineteen years to get out of high school, where all she had to do was to learn how to type. Her father is a gardener...

MARC : A landscape architect.

GERTRUDE : ... and her mother is a gambler from Brooklyn.

MAC : She plays bingo at the local church, and just happens to have been born in Brooklyn.

GERTRUDE : (*fiddling furiously with her beads*) The whole situation is ridiculous. I can't imagine what motivates you. I would say that this woman has charmed you out of your senses, if I believed for a moment that she had any real charm. Since she is all body and no mind, I can only assume that you are blinded by sheer animal lust. In which case you cannot expect from me approval, respect—or money.

MARC : Did it ever occur to you that I might love Laura Haley?

GERTRUDE : Never. And, what's more, I don't believe it's ever occurred to you either.

MARC : How do you know?

GERTRUDE : (*with a wise smile*) Because I know you better than you know yourself. Love has nothing to do with it.

MARC : Well, you couldn't be more wrong. I love Laura Haley and I'm going to marry her. How about that for filial defiance?

GERTRUDE : Then you leave me no choice. I will not see the family fortune squandered on a domestic tragedy, eaten up by legal fees and alimony. If you marry that wretched girl, I will disinherit you the day after the wedding.

She said something after that, but my ears were plugged up with rage and, in my mind, I saw blood running out of her mouth. In that instant, I knew I had no choice but to kill her.

Monday, 12 May

I walked to work along Eleventh Street, imagining that I could smell roasting coffee in the clear morning air. The concrete was hard but unreal. The various parts of my body seemed unrelated. I could not understand the signals that made my feet move. I looked down at them, mildly fascinated at the determination with which they carried me towards my office. The hand that carried my attaché case might have been a stranger's hand, stitched on to me by some mad scientist, who gathered my parts from a dozen different graves. It occurred to me that perhaps I had been drinking and smoking too much and that my brain was deprived of adequate oxygen. I renewed my promise that I would cut down.

I was pre-occupied all day with the problem of how to kill my mother. For a person whose life is essentially sedentary, it is not easy to think in terms of real violence. I have never held a gun in my hand. I have never drawn blood. I solve most of my problems in writing. I write memos. I type reports. I scribble. I fill out forms. If only I could handle my mother in the same way. If only I could fill out a form in triplicate that would remove her from the face of the world.

I could hold nothing clearly in mind all morning. Linda brought in coffee about ten and I merely stared into her bosom, as though I were being served by a pair of disembodied tits. At eleven there was a meeting in Leonard Pike's office. He is executive editor of the text division and a vice-president of the company. I have no idea what the meeting was all about. I chain-

27

smoked and looked from face to face. The voices I heard did not seem to correspond with the mouths that moved, as when the picture and sound fail to co-ordinate in a movie.

My mind wandered. It was full of violence. I saw myself on the cover of a suspense novel with a smoky revolver and a raincoat, standing over the half-nude corpse of my mother. I forced myself to think about knives. How would it feel to plunge a dagger into living flesh? Would it take much strength? And what, after the first stroke, if the subject does not die, but merely lies there on the bedroom floor, staining the polar bear rug and looking up at you with those martyr-mother's eyes?

Something Mr. Pike did brought to mind the guillotine. He hit the palm of one hand with the edge of the other, as though he were trying to karate it in two. I caught a few words about the revolution in higher education. And then I was off again, assaulted by visions of strangling, garrotting and axes plunging à la Dostoevsky into the greying heads of hateful old women. Visions of straight razors drawing across narrow white necks that smelled of soap and perfume as you hugged them from behind.

Then I was back in my green cubicle again, without remembering how I got there. And Linda was standing beside me with a steno pad, patiently chewing gum. Her skirt was cut off between her knee and hip, and for a moment my only link with reality was the nakedness of her thighs. I had to stifle an impulse to ram my hand up between those bare legs. 'Well?' she said in unadulterated Brooklynese. I looked puzzled. 'You buzzed, didn'tja?' I stared at her blankly. She's a plumpish girl with creamy skin and blonde hair that's dark at the roots. 'Never mind,' I finally said. She gave a vicious chew at her gum and said, 'Gee, I wish you'd make up your mind. I gotta meet my girl friend for lunch.'

I too had to meet my girl friend for lunch, but it wasn't quite the same. Laura, my girl bride. The woman who will save my sanity. The woman with whom I will live the good life. In an age of revolution, I am an ultra-conservative, a reactionary, perhaps even a fascist. I see the good life in antique terms. I envision a large house overlooking the sea, or perhaps a valley in which a small village is nestled. It is an old postcard village, a small cluster of houses with a church spire. It might be Swiss, English or even American. But the modern, carbon-monoxide world has not yet descended upon it. The silence is broken only by the sounds of nature. In the house, sun streams through large windows and falls on deep carpets. In the book-lined library, I sit at my desk smoking a pipe and writing. I write longhand and the words come to me like music. Later, the mail arrives and I have tea in the solarium as I go through it. I am surrounded by greenery and sunlight. The letters are from everywhere, from publishers and admirers. I am asked to do an autobiography, which I will politely refuse. I am asked also to make an appearance in New York, which I will say is impossible because I simply do not go to New York any more. Laura comes in and refills my cup. She sits opposite me at the glass-topped table. The sunlight reveals a few grey hairs, but she is at the height of her beauty. She reminds me that Hamilton Williams, the poet, is coming to dinner and that we are having coquille St. Jacques. The children are away at school, but will be home at the week-end. I am romantically stirred by the sight of Laura. I look at her and she knows the meaning of my look.

Laura is no intellectual giant but she has a kind of animal genius. Her life is governed autocratically from the Kremlin of her ovaries. She is all instinct—all female instinct. She will be a good mother without ever stopping to consider the problem of motherhood. In an age of sexual confusion and nervous women she is refreshingly atavistic. And though delicate in her proportions, she has the native strength of her sex. Like Faulkner's women, she will endure. She will tend to my needs as long as I can maintain my foothold in this precarious world and then she will lay me away in the ground and come from time to time with flowers and a simple prayer. About the giant issues of life, Laura has no opinions, except that she is sure there is a God. But her God is like the largest of the fuzzy toys she collects, a great cuddly teddy bear who will ward off the goblins of the night.

Laura is a virgin and it has never occurred to her to be anything else, until, as she so poetically puts it, 'the right man comes along'. She has assured me endlessly that I am the right man but we have agreed 'to wait for the proper time'. The choice is as much mine as hers. In fact, perhaps more mine than hers. I think the wedding night should be a ritual : the pure, pure virgin bride laid out on silken sheets like an antique sacrifice to a pagan god.

Laura works for a law firm called Rose, Rifkin, and Blau. Her immediate boss is Morton Rose, who, Laura says, changed his name from Mordecai Rosenberg. 'I guess it sounded too Jewish,' she explained. She is amused by his lecherous advances and talks freely about them.

When I met Laura for lunch today at Enrico's, the subject came up again. Smiling into her daiquiri, she said, 'That Mr. Rose is a riot.' I put down my martini and waited anxiously for her to go on. My eyes were focused on her dangling ear-rings. 'He says he wants to buy me a car but that I have to use it to drive to his summer place in Monticello.' Curses accumulated in my dry throat, but I swallowed them away. Then I said in my calmest voice, 'Are you sure you haven't done anything to encourage him?' She laughed away my question and then said, 'Oh he's harmless. Besides, he's almost forty.' In a near whisper, I reminded her that I was thirty-five. 'That's different,' she said. 'He's bald and married and all that.' I explained that married men were often the most dangerous. And for the next five minutes, I cross-examined her : 'Did he ever touch you, even accidentally? Does he use foul language? Do you sit immodestly when you take dictation? Does he stare at you? Does he touch himself or get excited when you're with him?'

She leaned back and sighed. 'Marc, stop it. You've got such a funny look on your face. Can't we talk about something else?'

I suddenly became conscious of myself. I was hunched forward. The muscles in my face were tight. And I was on the brink of sexual excitement. I desperately wanted to see myself in a mirror to reassure myself that I had not sprouted fangs or in some other way revealed the darker part of myself. I brushed back my hair, lit a cigarette, and forced myself to smile. 'I'm sorry,' I said. 'I didn't sleep well last night. I had a bad day yesterday.'

'It was Mother's Day,' she said, as though nothing bad could ever happen on Mother's Day. 'I thought you had dinner with your mother.'

'I did,' I said, 'but we had a terrible argument.'

'Oh? About what?' she said.

'About you,' I said.

She looked into her glass. 'I'm sorry she doesn't like me,' she said. 'But she hasn't really given me a chance.'

I reached across to touch her hand. She was toying unconsciously with her knife. Something in her gesture plunged me suddenly into a fantasy in which she was about to kill my mother. They were in a dungeon. Gertrude's hands were tied behind her. She was naked. The stone floor glistened with dampness. Into the flickering torchlight stepped Laura, naked also, except for a pair of black boots and a mask. She carried a whip in one hand and a dagger in the other. The whiteness of their bodies was very vivid, exaggerating the blackness of their pubic hair. Gertrude pleaded. And Laura said, in her girlish voice, 'That was a mean thing to do.' The whip came down on Gertrude's back. Then on her buttocks. Gertrude, lifting her eyes as though to heaven, let out a primeval wail. The whip descended again, leaving red tracks across her breast. 'I don't mind telling you,' said Laura in her inappropriate voice, 'that you're not a very nice person.' And the leather thongs ripped across Gertrude's belly, multiplying the old scar. She fell to her knees and looked up pathetically at the young girl who stood before her. Laura moved closer and put aside the whip. Her legs were spread apart, her patch of pubic hair almost in Gertrude's face. 'Mothers should not eat their children,' said Laura's high-school voice, disconnected now from the girl in the leather boots who leaned over the older woman. She untied Gertrude's hands. In an outburst of gratitude Gertrude stood up and threw her arms around Laura. The two women, their naked bodies pressed together, embraced for a long moment, sucking at each other's mouths, thrusting their hips forward. But the dagger was still in Laura's hand and I saw her raise it slowly behind Gertrude's back. As it plunged into her flesh, the dungeon went black and there was a crash that startled me back to reality. Apparently, my hand had drawn away suddenly from Laura's and I had sent a water glass tumbling to the floor.

When I lit a cigarette, I could see that my hand was trembling. Laura was distracted by the waiter who knelt beside her, stacking the broken pieces of glass.

31

I saw Popoff after work and told him about the incident. He did not comment directly. He sits with his back to the window and tends to disappear into a silhouette.

After a long pause he said, 'Why don't you make love to your fiancée?' There was something old world in his tone and choice of words.

'Why do you want to know?' I said suspiciously.

He didn't answer for a long time. I got impatient and then stiffened suddenly in the half-reclining leather lounge that faced partially away from him. 'Well, answer me, for Christ's sake.' I said angrily. 'Why is it that you never answer me when I ask you a question?'

'I thought you had something more to say,' he said calmly from his protected shadow. 'Or perhaps you'd rather not talk about it.'

I leaned back and thought for a moment. The question receded and I stared at the rows of books in the bookcase, tempted, for some reason, to count them. Time ticked away.

'Well?' he said, urging me back into the conversation.

I felt cornered. My voice went flat. 'Perhaps I'm romantic,' I said. 'I'd like her to be a virgin.'

'Always?' he said.

'Don't be ridiculous,' I said. I hesitated. 'I want to begin a new life. I want to do things the right way. If I made love to her now, it would ruin everything.'

'If you are going to marry her anyway, what possible difference can it make?' he said.

'She would lose her innocence,' I said. 'I want her to be innocent.'

'Would you lose your respect for her, if she went to bed with you?' he said.

'Respect?' I echoed. 'I don't know. I don't think of it in those terms. I don't want to make her unhappy.'

'Do you think it would make her unhappy if you made love to her?' he said. Out of the corner of my eye, I could see him lean forward and pick up something from the blotter on his desk. It was a letter opener in the form of a dagger.

I turned on him again. 'Look,' I said, 'I know what you're trying to get me to say. You want me to say that I associate sex with filth and that if I make love to Laura I will feel that I have soiled her.'

'No, my friend,' he said, 'not *soiled* her; *killed* her.' He raised the little dagger and brought it slowly down. 'You see,' he said. 'You plunge in your knife and they become helpless. When you are done, they are like corpses—at least in your mind.' He leaned back and let out a sigh of a laugh that reminded me, for some reason, of yellow teeth. 'Ah, but it is only symbolic,' he said, with a wave of his hand, as though brushing the whole matter aside.

I actually ate a TV dinner in front of the television set this evening, which is the way God intended it, I suppose. I suddenly became conscious of myself hunched forward on the hassock with my aluminium throwaway plate in my hand just under my chin and my half-rolled-up eyes gobbling in the seven o'clock news. I watch the news compulsively these days. I don't know why. It doesn't mean much to me. I don't even remember the names of the Secretary of State or the Secretary of Defence, though these shapers of our national destiny parade frequently enough in the unreal light of my television screen. I listen to the baseball scores with the same intense indifference that I view what seems to me the same film clip day after day of the Vietnam War.

After the news, I turned off the TV set. I took my notebook into the kitchen, where I find it easier to concentrate, and arranged myself at the red formica-topped table, pushing aside the toaster and sugar bowl. I felt for a moment like a schoolboy trying desperately to apply himself to his homework. I know I have to do this thing systematically. And I know that I have to be on guard against myself. A criminal is his own worst enemy.

I approached the problem in a business-like way, listing all the usual forms of murder. I could lure her to a remote spot somewhere and bash her head in with a rock; I could attach an explosive device to her car; I could hide in her apartment and strangle her in her bed; I could pick her off through the telescopic sight of a high-powered rifle; I could poison her; or I could take her out in the *Albatross* and drown her.

33

None of these schemes seemed very workable, however. They were too dramatic, borrowed mainly from the movies, where it is easy to commit murder. In real life it is much harder. If one has the normal range of sensibilities, one is appalled by death. One doesn't want to confront the person one has to kill. It is in that final confrontation that one is most likely to fail. I can see myself standing before Gertrude, perhaps in the living room of her apartment. I say to her, almost apologetically, 'I'm going to kill you now.' She doesn't believe me, of course, but there is something in my tone of voice that worries her. She walks away nervously, like Bette Davis, and says something like, 'You have a morbid sense of humour,' or 'Marc, darling, when are you going to grow up?' Something collapses inside of me, and instead of strangling her or plunging a dagger into her throat, I smile shyly and mumble something stupid that will indicate it was all a joke. No, I must not confront her that way. There must be no conversation, no discussion, no opportunity to back out.

I went to the window and looked out. I looked at other windows and down into the street. A taxi went by. An elderly man in a white shirt was walking his dog. It was a small quick dog, who lifted his leg at the base of the lamp-post. I looked for my Lady of the Geraniums. She's the woman in the window directly opposite me. I don't really know her, and, yet, in a way, I know her quite well. Sometimes she leaves the blinds open at night so that I can see in. I am sure that she knows when I am looking at her. I stand by the window purposely so that she can see me. I can watch her undress. She does it slowly, watching herself in her mirror. She unbuttons her blouse, revealing her bra. That first moment is very exciting. She drops her skirt and stands for a moment only in her underwear. She glances towards me but never offers a sign, no confirmation, no recognition, no connection at all. She reaches round and unsnaps the bra and hunches her shoulders to remove it. Her breasts are large and clearly visible as they catch the light of the lamp. Still in her underpants, she fusses with her hair. The blinds are set at such an angle that probably I am the only one who can see in. Finally, she removes everything, stepping long-legged out of the silk or nylon garment that shrinks to almost nothing once she is out of it. I call her my Lady of the Geraniums because she has them growing in a flowerbox on her windowsill. On weekends a man comes to visit her and she closes the blinds.

The days were getting very long. In my small stretch of sky, I could still see traces of light but the streets were dark. I sighed against the window and my breath made a dull spot that spread and then retreated again. It's a dreary time—I mean until the absolute night.

I felt myself sinking into boredom and despair. I picked up a copy of *Playboy* and studied the nudes. There was a cheerful young blonde with very pink nipples. She was bending over and I imagined taking her from behind and hefting her breasts. I remembered incidents from the past. I have stored up things and can bring them to life again at will. If I am ever imprisoned this ability will make my life bearable.

But I was not a prisoner yet. I was restless and full of animal longings. Perhaps I am a kind of werewolf after all. I went out and walked over to Fifth Avenue and then down to Eighth Street and then along Eighth to Sixth Avenue and then south towards the park. It was like a mid-summer night in the Village. The streets were full and the shops along Eighth Street were still open. I walked slowly, absorbing the girls. They were all around me— naked legs in mini-skirts, flashing leather boots, breasts moving loose and heavy behind shirts and blouses, the nipples erect and clearly visible through the material. I walked behind one, noticing the rhythm of her hips and how the net stockings disappeared up under her dress and between her legs. I walked past her, brushing her lightly on the crowded narrow sidewalk.

There was an odd tightness in my head as I hesitated at the corner, trying to decide which way to go. One way seemed as good as any other. For a moment I was dizzy and I thought my eyes might cross. But the feeling passed and I headed for the park.

I took the long way around and stopped for a glass of wine. I stood at the bar. In one of the booths, there was a Negro with a thin blonde girl. She had the desperate look of a nymphomaniac. Her skirt was very short. The Negro's eyes were large and his eyelids drooped. He had an Afro and a white turtleneck and looked a little faggish. I imagined that I might just walk over to them and whisper, 'Let's all go somewhere and fuck.'

In my mind, they smiled at me weakly, as if from another world or perhaps from the grave. They rose silently and we walked out single file and down the street to a half-ruined tenement house. We went into the dark hallway, first the girl, then me, then the Negro, shadowy. The darkness smelled of urine. We climbed some stairs and turned a key in a door on which there was no number. We lit a candle in a wine bottle and, in the flickering light, we lay down on a mattress on the bare wooden floor. Our clothes disappeared. The Negro had his fuzzy head between the girl's legs and she was writhing. He was on his knees, his lean hips in the air. I straddled the girl, so that when I looked down her head seemed to be growing out from between my legs. I had an urge to sit on her face, to crush her, to strangle her. Behind me I could feel her legs flying, as though she were trying to ride an invisible bicycle upside down. And then the Negro and I took turns, until she pleaded for us to stop. But we did not stop. I leaned over the sweating back of the Negro as he took his turn and whispered, 'Let's fuck her to death.'

I finished my wine and went up to Washington Square Park. It was crowded as usual, and everyone moved slowly, as if the place were too small for a brisk walk, or as though they were hypnotised by the oasis of greenery in the stone desert. The triumphal arch rose pointlessly into the night. The fountain was a mandala promising salvation to all the spaced-out young Christs. The children's playground was abandoned. Somewhere someone was playing a flute. There were ripples of sound, some occasional laughter, a voice calling across the dark lawn.

I sat beside a girl in a raincoat. She was trying to read by lamplight. She slouched and her legs were straight out and crossed at the ankles. Even in the darkness I could see that her sandalled feet were dirty. The raincoat had fallen away from her thighs, which were naked. She had on a pair of round over-sized glasses that had a yellow tint and made part of her face seem yellow.

I lit a cigarette and studied her surreptitiously. She ignored me, keeping her eyes fixed on her book. She seemed frozen into immobility. She did not even turn the pages. Finally, a breeze stirred her blonde hair. It blew across her face. Still she did not move. After a while I leaned towards her and said, 'What are you reading?' She looked at me with corpse-like coolness and said, 'I'm not reading! I'm meditating.' I slid closer and tried to see the title of the book, but it was upside down. 'I'm sorry if I disturbed you,' I said.

She started to talk in a peculiar monotone, as if she were talking to her feet instead of to me or anyone. 'You know it's like you fix your eyes on a point just short of the page so that it's all a kind of blur and your mind goes hazy and like after a while there's a little hum in your ear and the world around you starts to fade out.'

I asked her if she came to the park often and if she lived nearby and a few other dumb things but she didn't seem to be listening. 'It's a little hum like from hash and that square inch of space comes alive and you see all sorts of things in it like molecules and germs and the souls of people who died a thousand years ago in India and it makes your whole life a lot clearer and like more solid because you get away from just the surface of things and really into things and you find out how many different kinds of space there are.'

Our conversation was a counterpoint in which I went my way and she went hers. After a while, neither of us was listening to the other. I wanted to slap her across the face the way one does with people who are hysterical or in a state of shock. Instead, I stood up, took her by the arm and led her away. She came without resistance, as though she had understood my invitation when I said, 'Let's go to my place for a drink.' Her voice went on: 'Like freedom is an inside thing all in the mind and there are so many avenues you can go down and corners you can turn, like you know a labyrinth, so you wander into eternity and find out it's all like connected and nobody ever really dies but sort of goes in and out in time as if it was a big Swiss cheese . . .'

In my mind, I told her she was a big Swiss cheese and that I was going to go in and out of her before long. I felt the warm flesh of her arm through her raincoat as I led her home. It wasn't until we were in my apartment and she was sitting beside me on the couch with a glass in her hand that she looked up out of her trance for a moment and said, 'Where are we?' I told her but she did not react. She slipped away again and was talking about how nobody belongs to anybody and how in a thousand years we would all have collective minds. I took the glass out of her hand and undressed her. I put the cushions of the couch on the floor and led her to them. She was totally pliable. I arranged her on the cushions and then took off my clothes.

I indulged myself leisurely, amused by her detachment. Gradually, her voice grew fainter and more distant and once she paused, as though listening for a noise in an empty house. At last her body responded, though her voice remained disconnected to the bitter end. And even as she shuddered and sighed, she went on. 'Like deep down in the blood we know where life is and where it's going, and oh, like there's . . . oh baby, there's where like it's . . . oh . . . going to be . . . ah . . . like always.' And she slumped into a heap of silent flesh.

Tuesday, 13 May

I was late for work. The background noise of office machines and telephones seemed unusually loud. Linda brought me coffee and said that Hinkle wanted to see me. I scribbled his name on a memo pad and pushed it aside. I looked at my accumulation of work. The pile of papers grew higher every day. Behind me, on a shelf, manuscripts multiplied. I couldn't decide where to begin.

The calendar reminded me that it was the 13th of May. How was that possible? I wondered. It seemed to me that just the other day it was the middle of February and I was leaning into a cold wind and trudging through grey slush. And now it was almost the middle of May and I was supposed to be married on the 2nd of June. That gave me less than three weeks. Good Lord, less than three weeks to commit the perfect matricide. What could I have been thinking of. Even assuming that the deed could be planned and carried out in that time, how could I possibly have my wedding right on the heels of my mother's funeral. But perhaps I could arrange it so that her body was not discovered until after the wedding, or possibly not at all. But that means disposing of a corpse, a rather difficult chore in a place like New York. And the dead are so heavy to carry around. I had a fleeting vision of a bloody scene in a bathroom. I was cutting Gertrude's body into little pieces and flushing them down the toilet. I wondered if it had ever actually been done.

I returned to the *Albatross* scheme. Perhaps if she were drowned at sea she would never appear again, like my father.

They would search for her. There would be a lot of confusion and the wedding would have to be postponed. But would she be legally dead if they couldn't find her?

I thumbed my way into June and then July and August, turning the pages one by one, oddly fascinated by the progression, as though I were watching time itself ooze by. Then I felt an icy hand grip my groin and chills raised the skin on the back of my neck. In that instant, I knew that the passage of time was real and that there was nothing I could do to stop it. Eventually, I would be shoved out of life and into the past. We would all be shoved out. And I thought of all those young girls out there beyond my green cubicle, typing and chewing and dreaming of lovers and children.

I re-counted the days. The task seemed impossible. Perhaps Gertrude was unkillable, after all. A series of scenes clicked into my mind like slides going through an automatic projector. She was lying on the bed and I was strangling her. Othello and Desdemona. My knee was between her legs. I could feel her struggling thighs. It occurred to me in that moment that I could almost certainly throw the police off my trail by assaulting her sexually before killing her. Click. We were standing on a high promontory that looked out across the wild sea. I stood behind her. The wind blew in our faces as though we were posing for the dust jacket of a romantic novel. My hands were on her shoulders. God knows what we were saying to one another or thinking. I urged her forward. She turned suddenly and clawed at my face as she fell away into the whistling gale. Her pathetic scream was like a giant sigh, and I heard the fluttering ruffle of her petticoat.

'When in the chronicle of wasted time,' came a voice from the gale, 'I see descriptions of the fairest wights . . .' It was Virginia Workman standing in front of my desk and smiling down at me from behind her dark-rimmed glasses. 'You're reading that thing as though it were a suspense novel,' she said. She's a woman of thirty with a large mouth and a slightly double chin. She's fond of tight high collars and brooches and looks a little old-fashioned. I had heard that she was, until recently, a nun, and had given it up. We chatted. 'Come by after work for a

drink,' she said. Without thinking, I agreed and she went away
with a nervous smile.

I had lunch with Laura at a Greek restaurant called Milo's,
where the food is inexpensive and the noise-level is high. We
talked, smiled and held hands, but we could not hear a word,
which may not have mattered. Afterwards, I walked her back to
her office, kissed her, and watched the revolving door gobble her
into the dark and shiny guts of an office building.

The afternoon was flushed into the corporate plumbing with
meetings, forms, and telephone calls from worried pedants. Five
o'clock arrived with depressing suddenness.

It was not until I was in the elevator, pressed against the soft
body of one of the nameless girls from the seventh floor, that I
remembered Virginia Workman's invitation.

Poor Virginia must have run all the way, because by the time
I arrived she had already changed into less forbidding garments
and set out some bottles and glasses. She might have once been a
great nun but she was a lousy bartender, confusing rye for Scotch
and ginger ale for club soda.

We talked nervously for a while, obviously aware that we were
about to have an adventure. She kept poking at her glasses as
though they were going to fall off. Finally, she took them off and
put them down on the coffee table. Her eyes looked suddenly
smaller and somewhat unfocused, as though she had been drinking a great deal. She said she went to a Catholic college and spent
seven years in a teaching order. Disillusioned by their pettiness
and perversions, she left her sisters for the world beyond the wall,
where (she giggled hysterically) she found nothing but pettiness
and perversion.

I wandered about the room, looking at this and that, and saying the usual things. When I approached her where she sat on
the couch, she stiffened and leaned back. I sat down beside her
and said, 'I like you much better without your glasses,' which was
a lie. 'In fact, you're a very attractive woman.'

She looked at her hands. 'Actually, I was always the ugliest one in the family,' she said. 'I have a younger sister who is a real beauty.'

I touched her hair and face gently, reassuringly, and said in what might have been a priestly voice, 'People never see themselves as other people see them.'

I could see her chest going up and down and her eyelids fluttering. I waited for some kind of an Emily Dickinson response, but suddenly she fell towards me. Tears started to well up in her puffy lost eyes and she said, 'Nobody has ever made love to me and I'm thirty years old.'

'Incredible!' I said. After the first long hungry kiss we fumbled furiously for buttons, hooks, and zippers, and in a few minutes we were stark naked on the floor performing the oldest ritual in the world—the virgin's deflowering. In this case, the flower was a little wilted, but no flower is really ugly. It was a brief and rather formal ceremony. After a while, I could feel my forces gather, like a bow drawn back. But before the string was released, before the arrow was launched, the doorbell rang. Virginia leapt up and staggered around blindly. 'Just a minute,' she called out, and the bowstring went limp. She located her glasses and then she was able to say in a hoarse whisper, 'Take your things in there.' She nodded towards the bedroom. I obeyed sheepishly and scurried off with an armful of clothes, my necktie trailing. There was a draught between my legs, where my poor weapon had been dampened in more ways than one.

Through the keyhole of the bedroom door, I could see what was going on. Virginia (now in a bathrobe) was being visited by two black bats with pale faces framed in starched white linen. One had a squeaky Irish accent and the other was a contrapuntal contralto. At first, all three women talked at once and it was hard to tell what the nature of the conversation was. But then the Irish one (a diminutive woman and not unpretty) seemed to prevail. 'Mother Theodora wants you to come back,' she said. 'She has been praying very hard for you and has talked to Monsignor Flynn, who says it can be arranged.' Virginia said that she had just come out of the bathtub, as if this was of some theological importance. The other nun kept repeating, 'Remember your vows. Remember your vows.'

I stood up and wandered away, my back stiff from the awkward posture. I was still clutching my bundle of clothes, like a little boy looking for someone to dress him. I looked at the paintings on the wall and at the crucifix over the head of the bed and then glanced surreptitiously at myself in the mirror. When I turned around, it was to discover that my nightmare of being naked on stage had suddenly come true. Some draught, possibly the breath of God, had blown open the bedroom door and a silent, paralysed audience was staring at me from the next room.

I stepped forward and made a feeble gesture that was unaccompanied by words (what, after all, was there to say?). As I did so, one of my shoes fell and made a soft thud on the rug. I suppose my gesture was misinterpreted as an aggressive act and the contralto nun dropped to her knees and prepared herself for rape and martyrdom, her fingers doing double-time on her rosary beads. The Irish one stared at my naked maleness. Then her eyes shot to my feet suddenly, as though she were looking for a cloven hoof, and then snapped back to my groin, which obviously, in her mind, was the centre of my personality. 'My dear girl,' she said in a voice trembling with emotion. 'My dear girl.' She crossed herself twice and then launched into a frantic prayer. She dragged her kneeling colleague to her feet and supported her to the door. They disappeared like a bundle of black sheets and the door slammed behind them. Virginia disappeared into the bathroom, perhaps to pray, who knows. And I was left alone to consider my nakedness and the comic absurdity of life.

At home again, I watched the seven o'clock news. It kept interfering with my meditations on nuns, but I was unable to turn it off. Huntley and Brinkley, the one secretly sad, the other secretly angry, were so woven into my speculations that for a fleeting moment, I saw them in stiff white habits as Sister Chet and Sister David.

Why do I find nuns sexy? Perhaps it's because I am convinced that they are all lesbians and do bizarre things in their 'convent's narrow room'. I have always been fond of lesbians and the idea of two naked women embracing is exciting to me. I would like to watch them. I would like to see them press their mouths and breasts together.

For a few minutes, I was a ghost in a convent passing through stone walls into the secret rites of naked nuns, but the face of an English statesman appeared on the screen and I suddenly remembered that I was expected at Uncle Phil's for dinner at seven-thirty.

The invitiation from Uncle Phil was oddly coincidental with my decision to kill Gertrude. I have always had the feeling that Uncle Phil knows something important that I ought to know. My speculations, based on nothing whatsoever, lead in strange directions. Sometimes, I imagine that he and my mother conspired to kill my father and that they were—and may still be—secret lovers. But when I see him sitting in his leather club chair with his cigar in one hand and his brandy in the other and a benign smile on his round face that is repeated in the semi-circles of his chins, I cannot imagine that he ever had enough passion for either murder or love.

Uncle Phil lives with his daughter Emily in an antique apartment house with high baroque ceilings and ponderous woodwork. One might expect servants to appear out of the boar-hunt tapestry or the wood panelling, but there are none. Emily, who mysteriously lost her ability to speak as a child, keeps house for her father. She is a few years younger than I am and a little strange. She peers out at the world from somewhere inside of her body, as though she were trapped in a haunted house.

For dinner, we had marinated spare-ribs. I love spare-ribs, but whenever I eat them, I think of cannibalism. Uncle Phil seemed to be watching me very closely. For a moment or two, I felt like a character in one of those Greek myths who has been invited to dinner by the king only to be fed a casserole of his own children. Perhaps, I thought, these were the ribs of Laura Haley, at which I nibbled, an amusing scheme cooked up by Queen Gertrude and her fat lover.

Before dinner was over, it was clear that Uncle Phil had been discussing my impending marriage with Gertrude. From behind his wine glass, he said, trying to be nonchalant, 'I understand the girl is considerably younger than you.' I let a cannibalised bone fall on the graveyard of my plate and looked up at him. When I didn't answer, he cleared his throat and went on. 'I have never pretended to offer you fatherly advice, my boy, but, after all, I am your father's brother and all that. And marriage is a damned serious business. What I mean to say is it could ruin a man's life. On the other hand, of course, it could be a great blessing. My own, as you know, was something of a failure. And, at the risk of boasting, I might say that I am an expert on domestic agony.' We both glanced at Emily, who sat calmly before her untouched meal, her hands folded in her lap, her eyes fixed on the candelabra.

Old Polonius went on. 'Women are delightful creatures when they are happy but when they are unhappy, they will always find a way to force you to share their unhappiness. Women are instinctively affectionate, but they are also instinctively greedy and predatory. They will kill anyone who interferes with their nest-building.'

Emily went into the kitchen and my mother's brother-in-law and I went into the living room to talk and drink brandy. I accepted a cigar from him and we blew smoke towards each other as Uncle Phil continued his lecture on the facts of life. When I could stand it no longer, I squirmed in my seat and said, 'Look here, Uncle Phil, what exactly are you trying to tell me?'

'Well,' he said, coughing into his own smoke, 'the point is that your mother is terribly upset about your plans to marry this Laura girl. And, what's more, I can hardly blame her. From what your mother tells me she doesn't seem your type at all.'

'Uncle Phil,' I said, 'I'm thirty-five years old. Don't you think it's about time my mother allowed me to make my own decisions?'

He looked at me sleepily, as though he was trying to remember why I was there and then said, ambiguously, 'Your mother is a very remarkable woman.'

He did not stop talking until shortly after he fell sound asleep in his chair. Emily, who had rejoined us, took away his cigar and brandy as though she were performing an accustomed duty.

Left alone with Emily, I didn't quite know what to do. I stood up to leave but then noticed that my dumb cousin was staring at me with a wise Mona Lisa smile. She poured me some brandy and took a sip from my glass before handing it to me. For the first time, it occurred to me that she was a real human being and not a piece of furniture or an idiot. 'I'm sorry you can't speak,' I said. 'There is so much to talk about.' She shrugged her shoulders and lifted an eyebrow, as if to say, 'What the hell is there to talk about?' We sat down on the couch and I said I often thought about her and wondered what kind of a life she led. I paid her some compliments and brushed a few strands of hair from her eyes. She was blushing, but kept looking at me. 'Can you make signs?' I said. She nodded. I drew her towards me and kissed her playfully. We were children again, playing kissing games in the attic and under the cellar stairs, deceiving the grown-ups, deceiving Uncle Phil, who stirred, as though we were part of his dream. Emily laughed into my neck like a school girl. 'Would you like to make love?' I whispered into her ear, my voice quiet but serious. I meant what I said.

She stiffened and drew away, looking suddenly sad and much older.

'I'm sorry,' I said. 'That was foolish of me. I don't know what made me say that.'

She tried to smile, but I could see tears gathering within her. Her lips quivered and her eyes moved quickly.

I didn't know what else to say and I stifled an impulse to attack her, to tear off her clothes, to wound her. She looked helpless and her helplessness antagonised me.

She was, after all, a child. And I was the mad rapist about to assault her. I reeked of alcohol and tobacco. My teeth were stained. Blood dripped from my eyes. And I was all warts and poison.

She sat there, her body leaning away from me, but her eyes still fixed on my face. In that moment, she was the compendium of all suffering and abused women. She was Antigone and Hecuba, Mary, the mother of God and St. Catherine. She was a million peasant girls swept away on the shoulders of Vandals and Huns and Mongolian hordes. History organised itself around her and her little pubic constriction was, for an instant, the centre of the universe, and I was the ultimate criminal—lecherous, incestuous, murderous. I should have been a Viking or a Moorish pirate. God, how I would have torn asunder all the little sea-coast towns of that mother-of-us-all, the Mediterranean Sea.

After a clumsy silence, I said, 'It's late. I'd better go.'

She nodded and walked to the door with me. I looked at her once more and saw the family resemblance in her handsome face. She was practically my sister, I thought. What madness to approach her like that.

I walked home through empty streets frightened by the compulsions that seemed to be taking over my life. Perhaps, against my will, I would one day do something awful and then someone would kill me. Yes, I would be killed—should be killed. And my heart galloped in my chest and made me dizzy.

Wednesday, 14 May

Three days have passed since Mother's Day and I have not even developed a clear approach. Perhaps I should just walk up to her in the street, stab her to death and then head for the nearest subway. In New York, the whole incident might go unnoticed. Or perhaps, to spare myself the agony of that last contact, I should hire someone to do it, a professional killer, like calling in a plumber or an electrician. Are they unionised? I wonder. The American Federation of Necrotechnicians.

I stayed in my cubicle all morning, trying to catch up on back work and trying to avoid Hinkle, who has been watching me all week. Neither of my efforts met with much success. My pile is immense, perhaps eight or ten inches high now. Buried in there somewhere are unmailed contracts for such thrilling projects as *The Anatomy of the Freshman Research Paper*. Much of the correspondence is from irate and impatient authors. Much of it is inter-office: forms that I seem unable to decipher, memos from production reminding me of deadlines that I will never be able to keep, unless by some magic I can figure out how to move back and forth in time, invitations to conventions that are already hangovers and disappointments to the little teachers who fled from their wives to attend them. The whole thing is too ridiculous to take seriously, and yet I am afraid to quit. And it's not just because of the money.

Harvey Hinkle, PhD, is in charge of texts for College English courses. He is an unconvincing character—I mean in the literary sense. But here he is, alive and well, lording it over me at Ransom-McKenzie with his little eyes and his big PhD. At thirty-two his hair is already growing thin and his face is grey but he is obviously destined to live forever.

After the coffee wagon had been around, he came into my cubicle with a steaming paper cup in his hand. 'How's it going?' he said with simulated cheerfulness. I leaned back executive fashion and I could tell that he did not much like standing in front of my desk like an office boy. 'I had a call from Rudolph Kuntz,' he said. For a minute, I couldn't remember who Kuntz was or what he was writing for us. 'Is that right?' I said. 'How is old Rudolph?' 'Old Rudolph is furious,' said Hinkle. 'You promised him galleys by April, and here it is May and the manuscript is still sitting on your desk.' I frowned, trying to remember what the book was called. 'All right, I'll call Kuntz and tell him I'm sorry. What more can I do?' Hinkle stepped back and looked at me. He stared long enough to make me uneasy. 'What's the matter?' I said. 'Oh, nothing, nothing,' he said. 'I'll talk to Pike about it.' I glared at him. 'What do you mean you'll talk to Pike about it? About what?' I said. 'About Kuntz,' he said. 'Whatever he decides is all right with me.' I returned to my work as if to dismiss him and Hinkle went out, a rose of anger in his pale cheek.

Laura called and said she couldn't make it for lunch. I was glad. I went down to Eighth Street alone and looked for a cheap place to eat. Afterwards, I browsed in the Marboro Book Shop, thumbing mostly through photography annuals and picture books about women and old movies. A girl in a very short skirt came in. I browsed my way towards her and then as I passed her I touched her with the back of my hand. Her flesh was soft under the yellow cotton. I stood beside her for a while, pretending to be interested in a bulky book on Eastern European economics, which was being offered to the world for the ridiculous price of forty-nine cents. The book did not tempt me, but she did. I could smell her clean flesh. I surreptitiously eyed her and imagined putting the whole palm of my hand against her buttock. She ignored me, lost in a volume of Degas prints. I should have said something, I suppose, but I really had no desire to talk to her. It was something of an impasse and after a while I was relieved when she moved away. She had a delicate face and long blond hair.

In the afternoon, Laura called to say that Gertrude had invited her over for lunch to discuss what she called 'something very important for all of us'. 'I should have called you first,' said Laura, almost in tears, 'but she asked me not to. She said there are certain things that women must keep to themselves.' I could guess instantly the nature of their conversation and was furious at Gertrude for subjecting Laura to such embarrassment. 'She said I have no right to marry you,' said Laura. 'She said I would ruin both our lives. She said you are not really the person I think you are and that I don't really know you at all.' If Gertrude were in the same room with me at that moment, it would have been an easy matter to kill her. I tried to comfort Laura, to tell her not to listen to anything that malicious woman said but she went on as though she didn't hear me. 'And then she said that you didn't really love me, that you only wanted me because I was young and pretty and would be nice to have around the house, like a piece of furniture.'

I told Laura that it was all sheer nonsense but that I didn't want to talk about it on the phone. 'Come to my place later,' I said, 'around six-thirty, I can't get away before then.'

At five o'clock, I rode uptown on the subway for my regular appointment with Popoff. It was an interesting session. We talked about exhibitionism but I can't recall exactly what Popoff's point was. I told him about my Lady of the Geraniums but not about an incident at the beach last summer.

When Laura arrived, I comforted her, using such words as *frustrated, jealous* and *possessive* to describe Gertrude. With such language it did not take long to exhaust the subject. I fixed us a drink and some sandwiches and we watched television for a while. Sitting on the couch we nibbled and nuzzled and hugged as though it were Saturday night at the movies in Smalltown, America. After a while, I felt myself getting excited and I tried to inch away from her but we were so entangled that however I moved I seemed to get closer to her instead of further away. She kissed me playfully on the cheeks and chin and as she did so, I could feel the pressure of her elbow in my lap. Then our mouths were together and her lips parted. I could feel that her warm breath was irregular and she pressed herself against me and squirmed as though she wanted to break out of her clothes. I think it would have taken only a word or two of whispered argument to have her naked in bed. With the iron of her will softened in the furnace of her body, all I had to do was to let the hammer fall. But I resisted the temptation and fumbled for a cigarette to break the spell. Laura looked disappointed, but what, after all, could she say? Though it pinched and itched, she was girdled in goodness and had to agree with my suggestion that it was time to leave.

After Laura was gone, I called my mother, planning to scold her, but I was met with such a barrage of sweetness and chatter that I decided to postpone the confrontation, and, instead, invited her to have dinner with me tomorrow night at the Coach House.

Thursday, 15 May

I woke up this morning agitated. I could remember none of my dreams. Nor could I remember what Laura looked like. This momentary obliteration of the girl I presumably loved filled me with waves of compassion. I wanted to call her up. I wanted to rush out to Long Island to see her, to comfort her, as though I had done her a great wrong. I checked the time. It was too late; she had already left home.

At the office, I was too distracted by the noise of business to call. Hinkle kept passing by my cubicle and peering in at me. He had the surreptitious glance of a movie-toilet creep. And Linda, her mouth full of gum and her sweater full of Linda, kept appearing with annoying requests. 'Mr. Porter wants to know have you got the line drawings for the Feldman.' And her hips would be in perpetual motion, as if she had to go to the little girls' room or had unbearably hot pants. I was tempted to leap on her right there, tear off her sweater, release those baby-fat boobs and screw her across my cluttered desk. I could imagine the buzzing crowd gathered at the door of my cubicle, the way they did that time when Mary Watson fainted.

Shortly before noon, Leonard Pike asked to see me. As a vice-president he rates a corner office with windows on two sides. A fancier version of the same office, on the top floor, belongs to our invisible president. Pike is almost sixty, a fatherly figure with abundant white hair and suspenders. He belongs to an earlier era, a time when publishing was the last refuge of the intelligent gentleman, the lad with the Princeton degree and basically no talent, except a knack for holding his liquor, and possibly a congenial though directionless sense of humour. Pike is guarded by an old harpy of a secretary named Tess. She is wiry and weasel-eyed and too old even for bitterness. I like to imagine that forty years earlier she was his mistress, but I can't think of her as young. As she led me into the inner chamber, she gave me a mournful look, as if to say, 'Everybody dies, and now it's your turn.' She would have done well during the French Revolution.

Pike motioned me to a chair beside his desk. He gave me a firm paternal lecture on how I had been neglecting my work. I did not try to explain why. As I got up to go he said, 'I don't have to tell you that Hinkle is down on you, but I'm willing to give you a chance to work things out.'

I thanked him and left. *Hinkle is down on you* echoed in my mind and back in my cubicle, I imagined the little near-sighted bastard on his knees in front of me. He was Claggert the sadistic homosexual, and I was Billy Budd, blond and beautiful.

By lunchtime, I had dismissed the whole incident from my mind and turned to thoughts of my motherless, jobless future. I had lunch with Paul Garrison of the trade department and a hairy expatriate writer. Paul Garrison and I have cigarettes, martinis and probably bad circulation in common. Almost everyone else on the staff at Ramson-McKenzie is dieting and jogging, a bunch of terrified little men, who imagine they can outmanœuvre fate by lifting dumb-bells or taking up golf. Paul is an ageing cocksman and a thorough ham. He plays the old-style editor, the literary midwife, 'without whom,' as so many dedications have pointed out, 'this book could not have been written'. He travels to London and Paris and exotic places like Mallorca and Crete. He is referred to by name in *The Saturday Review.* He was a friend of Hemingway's and once met T. S. Eliot. He is the only man at Ransom-McKenzie I really like, though his whole manner reminds me that I am not a part of the literary world, that great world of sensitive, desperate, drunken, poetic men, and wiry lesbian ladies with three names and unshaven armpits. That's the world I really belong in.

The writer's name was John Bogan. He had a beard and yellow teeth and had lived a long time in North Africa and the Greek

Islands. He spoke about Athens and Beirut and Tangier the way I might have talked about Boston or Philadelphia. He and Paul discussed friends they had in common and I felt a little out of it. Patiently and silently, however, I plotted my revenge in terms of a giant best-seller that would catapult me into instant international fame. One day, these two men would meet again, perhaps in London or Paris. They would say, 'Have you seen McMann's latest?' or 'Do you remember the day we had lunch with Marc in New York?' One day, I am sure, I will graduate from obscurity and invisibility and exist for real in the eyes of other people. I am tired of this shadowy and surreptitious life.

Gertrude kept me waiting for twenty minutes at the Coach House. When she walked in, I was staring into my martini, rehearsing my reprimand. I knew it was she while she was still an unfocused white linen blur. And then it happened. The skies parted. A chorus of angels filled the room with celestial music. And the sign for which I had been waiting for so long issued out of heaven. An inner ejaculation of joy thrilled my guts as the *New York Times*, which Gertrude clutched to her bosom, whirled into focus. O *Deus ex machina*! O happy revelation! In that instant my problem was solved. My mind galloped ahead: I saw the exchange of letters, the disguise, the false documents, and the vile deed itself, almost certainly strangulation. In my exuberance and relief, I stood up and embraced my mother, who retreated a step as though she were being attacked. I actually kissed her on the cheek and then watched the pieces of her momentary panic collect themselves into a calculated, smiling mask of maternal appreciation.

I relieved her of her burdens and sat down in the dim coolness of the windowless room. 'Have you placed your ad for a caretaker yet?' I asked, nodding towards the *New York Times*. 'It begins tomorrow,' she said, 'and runs for three days. I do hope I can find a reliable man. Lloyd Harbor is not what it used to be and I hate to have the place empty so much of the time.'

Oh you will find him all right, I thought, because I will be your man, old girl. I will be your reliable man, your caretaker. You can rely on me to take care of everything.

And then, as though I had two heads, two things happened at once. While I carried on a normal conversation with Gertrude, my mind galloped away into the badlands of fantasy.

GERTRUDE : I hope I can find someone who knows something about gardening. I'd be willing to pay him more, of course. I'd like to get the roses trimmed and the grape arbour repaired. There's so much to be done.

MARC : Good men are hard to find. With all this prosperity and democracy nobody wants to be a servant.

GERTRUDE : Well, he needn't think of himself as a servant. He would be a—a—an estate manager or something. I would treat him as an equal. Well—almost as an equal.

MARC : And, of course you can offer him the cottage.

GERTRUDE : Yes, that's exactly what I had in mind, though I was hoping to save it for you. I know how much you've always loved the cottage. When you were a little boy and the cottage was only a cabin, you used to say you would live there when you grew up. You said you wanted to grow a beard and write books and carve a big stick to walk with

I will serve you and service you madam cock of your walk and tender of your tender grapes and goatherd-swineherd rolling in the mud with your pigs and horny as your goats a man with a thousand talents and a dagger strapped to his leg like a gypsy no, not a gypsy but a gentleman with a little derringer and a mysterious Mississippi riverboat past, reformed by a lady evangelist in New Orleans and winner of a duel with a Faulknerian octoroon my own son by another marriage in another country a long time ago and besides the wench is dead as you will be after the proper application with everything in triplicate except the assassination itself which need only be a final hug around the throat and pressure in the right spot so that no noise is possible only a trail of documents and photographs of who of what invented man what fantasy-murderer what surrogate for this prince of darkness perhaps a black man all Uncle Tom on the outside but Black Panther on the in the woods. But now I suppose you won't really need the cottage, will you?

MARC: Not unless you change your mind about Laura.

GERTRUDE: I would only be lying if I said I approve. I don't approve, and eventually you will see why. By then, of course, it may be too late.

MARC: Laura was very upset by what you said to her yesterday. You must have been very hard on her.

GERTRUDE: I just wanted to explain my position in all this. Don't you understand? I'm not trying to be malicious, dear. After all, I am involved, you know. You are my only child, and the heir to everything we own. I have a responsibility to see to it that this dwindling family goes on and flourishes. In my old age, I would like to be surrounded by grandchildren. I have always imagined that when I got too old to be entirely independent that you would take over and look after me and the family property.

MARC: I may grow old before you do, at the rate we're going. I'm aging twice as fast as you are.

GERTRUDE: It's because you don't live properly. You don't

inside humming Ole Black Joe in the cotton field and fixing up your roses and dahlias nodding and bowing with pearly white teeth to the madam but crawling up the trellis one night to rape and stab white lady colonialist sahib and carve hate mottoes on her breasts and belly announcing liberation and death to tyrants secretly a white lord under the black slave who in a fairy tale emerges when magically kissed or blessed or recognised in some way by a queen no longer the warty ugly toad croaking away his life in lily-pad slime despised by a world that knows he belongs in shady realms and croaks his song for Satan and frightens the peach-white breasty princess whom he loves but so secretly that nothing can be read in his dumb sad eyes except that he is the victim of witchery and black magic and unfortunate circumstances like the handsome man you are destined to meet according to my crystal ball one to whom the fates have been unkind or else he might have been a senator at least or an elegant colonel in her majesty's royal houseguard horseless and harmless now but promising service and a touch of class worthy of an interview take care of yourself. You should give up smoking. It's an ugly habit anyway. It leaves a foul odour about the house. I keep complaining to your Uncle Phil, but he doesn't listen.

MARC: Speaking of Uncle Phil, you weren't thinking of writing his daughter into your will, were you?

GERTRUDE: I'd rather not say. There are several possibilities and variables.

MARC: What do you mean?

GERTRUDE: Well, you may decide, after all, not to marry; and, on the other hand, *I* may decide to re-marry.

MARC: After all these years?

GERTRUDE: Why not? I'm not exactly senile yet. And if you can go off and make a life of your own, I don't see why I can't.

MARC: What lucky fortune-hunter did you have in mind?

GERTRUDE: Don't be cruel. Besides, what I have in mind is my own business, isn't it? Let's talk about something else. Let's talk about food.

and references with passport photos and meticulous penmanship to make you love him and want him so that he can enter your life legally in order to deprive you of it with swift delicacy and appropriate apologies sorry madam but I am going to kill you now and time is short so we will dispense with the usual formalities and do only the necessary things if you will just remove your clothes and lie still while I sharpen the knife to make it all polite and painless a neat little plot to protect your son from maternal abuse and guarantee that certain inalienable rights will be his for ever and ever amen in the heavenly light of primogeniture which promises that the balls of the father will descend to the first born and shall not be devoured by one's mother under any circumstances however unfortunate the punishment for which shall be death by fire or strangulation at the hands of the handsome caretaker who shall gain entry by certain deceptions acquired in wartime in the service of her majesty the queen.

Friday, 16 May

I spent all morning in a business-like posture at my desk but I
was actually inventing my mother's murderer. My plan is quite
simple. I will answer Gertrude's ad in a manner enticing enough
to make an interview inevitable. I will provide her with complete personal data, letters of reference, and photographs. These
must be found in her possession later on. I will have to impress
myself upon the doorman, elevator operator and probably a number of other people. Perhaps I will have to establish a temporary
residence, so that when the investigation is carried out the trail
will lead clearly to me. Several people will have to confirm the
fact that I did, indeed, have an appointment at such and such
an hour, precisely the time, the autopsy will reveal, when the
murder was committed. Having fooled everyone else, I will not
necessarily have to fool Gertrude, though this might make the
whole thing easier. Once I am in her apartment, it won't matter
if she sees through my disguise because in another instant she'll be
dead. I'll grab her by the throat and cut off her rhetoric along
with her air supply and that will be that. There will be some
black days, of course, but the dawn will come eventually and the
sun will rise on my new life.

All morning, I wrestled with the problem of who the caretaker
should be. It was like creating a character in a novel. To be convincing he has to be complete. The author must know him
thoroughly, even though in the final manuscript details are selec-
tively revealed. I took notes on a yellow pad with a set of proofs
beside me, pretending to be deep in editorial work. I scribbled
names and statistics and even a few crude sketches.

A small army of wayward men vied for the position in my mind: ex-priests and athletes, retired businessmen and army officers, reformed alcoholics and ex-convicts. But none of them seemed exactly right.

I picked up the *New York Times* and read through the ad again: 'Caretaker. Reliable man with references needed to maintain small Long Island estate. Experience preferred. Small cottage provided.' I thought of *Lady Chatterley's Lover*. There is something inherently exciting about a male caretaker on a lady's estate, a man withdrawn into himself, into his final fortress, with nature a kind of moat between himself and the world.

My man would have to be very special, I decided. One cannot assign such an important task to just anyone. It would have to be a role that I enjoyed playing, a role in which I could abandon myself and, hence, be thoroughly convincing.

I was thumbing idly through the pages of the *Times*, still wondering, still searching, when at about eleven-forty-five I slipped into a profound mist, a kind of trance, and began to tremble all over. My head contracted with periodic spasms of pain. Two minutes later, at exactly eleven-forty-seven, Claude Elmath was born. He was no squealing, strangling infant, of course, but a dignified man of fifty-five, rescued from oblivion, from the grave, as it were. A man old enough to be my father and yet the child of my imagination. What a stroke of genius!

Though surely an inspiration, Claude Elmath did not materialise out of nothing, He was the offspring of a happy union between an advertisement for *Hamlet* and a picture of Commander Whitehead peddling Schweppes, both of which appeared on the same page of the *Times*. What a remarkable machine the mind is. It gobbled up these isolated items, combined them with God knows what storehouse of data and spewed out all the right answers. Click, flash, tick, tick, tick, went the machine with all the excitement of a pinball game and out came Claude, bearded, British and dignified, with a name worthy of a devilish crosstick inventor, an anagram of Hamlet plus Uncle Claude. The whole rotten family rolled into one—son, father, uncle—and all appropriate to mother Gertrude, who might also have been murdered had her son not been crippled by indecision. What sport!

What fun! What a marvellous trick! This meteor-man of mine, this fiction, will flash into existence 'strut and fret his hour upon the stage', and then disappear as simply as he arrived. The perfect crime, a crime committed by a man who does not exist and hence, cannot be caught.

It is a beautiful deception but I must be very careful. I must think it all through. Whatever documents I produce must be thoroughly convincing. In the minds of the police, Claude Elmath must live. They will hunt him down. They will study his habits, speculate about his origins, wonder who his friends are (I must remember to make some friends). But they will be stalking a phantom, a man immune to all their detective devices, a man without fingerprints or a mirror image, a kind of vampire who will disappear into the security of his grave once his grim business is done.

I left my office shortly after noon, too flushed with excitement to think of food or even to talk to anyone. I wandered up Fifth Avenue, without knowing exactly where I was going. I looked in the windows of men's clothing stores. I studied the faces of bearded men who went by. I consulted the *Yellow Pages* for theatrical wig-makers. But I have made no inquiries as yet. I must not use my own name. I can not use my regular handwriting, or even my own typewriter when I answer the ad. God, how much planning is required in these things! One has to be an absolute genius to commit murder successfully.

I was exhausted and distracted by the time I met Laura for dinner. She was in her usual Friday night good spirits. She chatted girlishly about the petty politics of her office and about all the things she had to do over the week-end. And then she moved, with all the irresistibility of the life force, to the subject that absorbed most of her waking hours—her wedding. She referred to it as *her* wedding. Even I, for some reason, thought of it as *her* wedding. I was only lending myself to the occasion because it would be ridiculous for her to stand at the altar alone.

But the wedding night, that was another matter. That would be *my* ritual, my black mass, and our roles would be reversed.

Laura would be the passive initiate. I would be the hooded priest with the jewelled dagger. I would lead her through the forest of the male kingdom to the castle of obedience and teach her, on her knees, to recite prayers of the flesh.

It was quite late when we got back to my apartment, but Laura did not seem eager to leave. She was preoccupied and serious. Her face was a little flushed. I made us a drink and we settled down on the couch for what I assumed would be the usual fifteen minutes of pre-goodnight pecking and mumbling, after which I would either take her to the train station or drive her out to Garden City. But tonight was different. The scene that followed I prefer to record without comment.

(As the curtain goes up we find Marc and Laura seated side by side on the couch. There is a coffee table in front of them, on which there is an ashtray, two drinks and a copy of *Playboy*, which Marc has forgotten to hide. Laura takes a long drink from her glass and then leans away from Marc to examine him thoroughly, as if she is seeing him for the first time. She looks at the magazine and then back at him.)

LAURA : Do you like to look at other girls?

MARC : Not especially. Why?

LAURA : (She picks up the magazine) Is this what all the bachelors read?

MARC : (laughs), Oh, some friend of mine left that here. It's not very interesting.

LAURA : Do you mind if I lock at it?

MARC : Of course not. (They move together and turn through the pages.) Some of the girls are really quite pretty. This one for instance.

LAURA : (studies the picture meditatively) I don't know how they can do that. I mean pose like that without any clothes. I'd be embarrassed to death.

MARC : Some girls like to be looked at. In fact, all girls like to be looked at. It's human nature.

LAURA : (finishes her drink and sounds soft and sleepy) I guess so. (Marc puts his arm around her and she looks towards him longingly. They kiss. The magazine falls to the floor.) Oh,

61

Marc, I do love you. I wish we were already married and settled down.

MARC : We will be soon, sweetheart.

LAURA : Sometimes I get so confused.

MARC : About what, darling?

LAURA : Oh, about sex, I guess. I mean there's so much of it around these days. You can't go to the movies without somebody taking off their clothes. And then all my friends talk about their adventures. You'd think they'd be ashamed of the things they do, but no, they're actually proud.

MARC : What exactly do they do?

LAURA : Oh, you know, they do it with boys they hardly know. Some of them have been doing it since they were thirteen. This girl Alice says she's done it with about twenty different boys. Can you imagine? They say I'm old-fashioned and silly.

MARC : Well, don't you listen to them, baby. You've got something they haven't got.

LAURA : I guess so. Still, sometimes I wonder. I mean we're practically married. And then I read this book. It's very interesting. It's called *A Manual of Modern Marriage*. And— (rattles the ice cubes in her empty glass) could I have another drink?

MARC : (leaps up) Sure! (goes out to the kitchen and returns with a shaker full of something. Pours them both a refill.)

LAURA : Anyway, it says a lot of things that make you think.

MARC : Like what?

LAURA : It says, for instance, that sometimes it's better to sleep together before you get ·married, so that you can find out whether or not you're compatible. They keep calling it *intercourse*, which I think is a horrible word. Anyway, they think that people should do it to sort of try it out.

MARC : You don't feel that way, do you?

LAURA : No, of course not. Do you?

MARC : I'm old-fashioned too. I think a girl should be a virgin when she gets married. A man likes to begin at the beginning, if you know what I mean.

LAURA : But it's not the same for men, is it?

MARC : Sometimes.

LAURA : (after a longish pause) I promised I would never ask about your past, but I don't suppose it's that way for you. I mean, being older and all. You don't have to say anything if you don't want to. I was just wondering.

MARC : No one ever meant anything to me until I met you.

LAURA : (pulling away a bit) Then there *were* others.

MARC : No one important.

LAURA : But someone.

MARC : (looks apologetic) Laura, I'm thirty-five years old.

LAURA : (leans against him again) I'm sorry. I've always known really. It doesn't make any difference. (They kiss. Laura pulls away suddenly.) Did you do it right here in this apartment? Maybe right here on this couch?

MARC : Do what?

LAURA : You know, make love to all those other girls.

MARC : (laughs at her) There weren't *all those other girls,* just two or three since I was in college but I never really got involved.

LAURA : Oh! (offers him her empty glass. He fills it from the shaker, and also his own.)

MARC : They were just—just friends.

LAURA : (They kiss for a while hotly. Then Laura pulls away with a shiver and stands up.) Ooo!

MARC : What is it, baby? What's wrong?

LAURA : While you were kissing me, I was imagining that you were kissing another girl, right here on the couch. And—and that's not all?

MARC : What do you mean?

LAURA : I mean you weren't only kissing her. For a minute, I could actually see you. It gave me such a strange feeling. (She drinks.)

MARC : (standing now beside her with his arm around her shoulders) You mustn't feel that way, sweetheart. I've led a very normal life, honest.

LAURA : May I have a cigarette please?

MARC : But you don't smoke.

LAURA : (getting just a little high) I know, but I would like a cigarette anyway.

MARC: (obliging her, gives her a cigarette and lights it for her. She puffs at it as one might imagine. She walks back and forth without saying anything, as though she is thinking or imagining things again.)

LAURA: I could actually see you with this other girl—naked, I mean. Where was it? Right here or in the bedroom?

MARC: I don't remember.

LAURA: Probably the bedroom. I mean, after all, if you're a bachelor and you have a bedroom, you might as well use it. (She's not really angry, just restless and curious and excited.)

MARC: You certainly didn't expect me to live like a monk all those years, did you?

LAURA: (finishes her drink again and helps herself from the shaker) Of course not, darling. I understand.

MARC: (sits down) Do you really?

LAURA: (with exaggerated softness) Of course I do, darling. (Comes to him and sits on his lap, draws his head into her bosom.) Sometimes you must really get—you know, you must really want to—I mean, I understand how men have to get rid of what's in there. And sometimes I think we are foolish to wait. Sometimes I would like to do it—I mean for your sake, darling. I know what you must be going through. It would make you feel so much better.

MARC: In a way, I guess. But . . .

LAURA: (smothering him somewhat) Poor Marc. You're so good to me. You're so—so—unselfish. I love you so much that sometimes I think I should do it. I mean, if it's what you want or what you need. If you really needed me.

MARC: No, Laura, I couldn't let you do that.

LAURA: Why not?

MARC: You might be sorry afterwards. It might spoil things for you.

LAURA: I don't see how. I don't know why it should spoil anything. Besides, who would know?

MARC: (Very uncomfortable, reaches around her for his drink and purposely spills it on her.) Oh my God, all over your dress.

64

LAURA : (Stands up abruptly and brushes at her dress.) Oh, damn. I hope it doesn't stain.

MARC : (standing and examining her dress) I'm sorry, honey. The glass was wet and . . .

LAURA : Oh, it's all right. It's a stupid dress anyway.

MARC : (looks at his watch) Oh my goodness, it's later than I thought. We've got to think about getting you home.

LAURA : But I'm not going home. I told my mother I might stay over with Jennifer.

MARC : But isn't it too late to go to Jennifer's?

LAURA : It doesn't matter. I told Jennifer that I would probably go home.

MARC : (puzzled) Then where *are* you staying?

LAURA : Well, I thought maybe I would stay here if you didn't mind. I could sleep on the couch or something . . .

MARC : Of course. But, you'll have to use the bedroom. I wouldn't consider putting you on the couch.

LAURA : (examining the empty shaker of drinks) You'll be sorry when you wake up in the middle of the night with a stiff back. Oh, we seem to be out of lemon punch, or whatever that beautiful drink was.

MARC : (firmly) Oh no, Miss Haley. (Takes the shaker out of her hand and puts it down) You've had enough for one night. It's past your bedtime. (Turns her round and urges her towards the bedroom. She resists playfully.) Now you go in there and get undressed. You'll find some pyjama tops in the bottom drawer of the bureau.

LAURA : But I don't want to go to bed. I want some lemon punch.

MARC : (He turns her round to kiss her good night and she flings her arms around him. He has to tear himself away and turn her again towards the bedroom. She goes off with a comical pout. He pats her bottom.) Good night, sweet dreams.

LAURA : Good night.

MARC : (Goes to a closet and takes out a blanket. Then he turns out all the lights and undresses. For a moment he stands completely naked looking towards the bedroom door. He lights a cigarette in the darkness. He gets under the blanket on the couch. In another minute the bedroom door opens and an angle of light cuts across the living room. Laura appears in her slip.)

LAURA : I can't find any pyjamas.

MARC : Look again. In the bottom drawer, on the right.

LAURA : Oh (goes out again and closes the door. In a few seconds she comes back minus her slip, wearing only panties and bra.) I found them. They're awful. After we're married, I want you to get a new pair.

MARC : After we're married, I won't need them. Now go to bed.

LAURA : (giggles and goes out again. In a few minutes she reappears in just the pyjama tops, but they are not buttoned.) They're not only ugly, but they are much too big for me. See. (She spreads her arms like a scarecrow, revealing her nakedness.)

MARC : You're going to bed, not to a fashion show. Now get in there and let a man get some sleep.

LAURA : (sadly and seriously accepts defeat) All right, all right. You sound like an old married man already. (She goes out.)

MARC : (Waits a moment. Puts out his cigarette and gets up cautiously. He approaches the door, kneels down and looks through the keyhole. What he sees can not be dramatically displayed without removing one wall of the bedroom. Laura is studying herself in the mirror. She turns this way and that and then removes the pyjama tops. She touches her hair and then her shoulders and breasts. Her hands linger there, squeezing gently, cupping her firm flesh. Her nipples are erect. Marc has to control his breathing. Laura tests the bed with her hands and then flings herself down on it with rough abandon. She does not pull back the covers. She spreads her legs and arms as though she is trying to fly. She draws up her knees and spreads them wide apart. She touches herself, moving rhythmically and as if in a dream. Marc feels her rhythm and echoes it. They are alone but together. And he kneels like a supplicant in the darkness. The keyhole is his connection with eternity. For a moment he is complete, immortal, the God of darkness witnessing his own creation. He opens and closes his eyes. He sees Laura. He sees the blazing sun. He sees Laura. He sees the breasts of a giant goddess. He sees Laura. The sea

66

wells in him, rocks him. The hum and sigh of his primitive beginnings is in his ears. He reels and falls away from the pinpoint of light. There is a lapse. He finds himself on the couch, trembling under the cover. He realises that he has fainted or blacked out. He can not tell for how long. He curls into a foetal position and wills himself to sleep.)

Saturday, 17 May

I sent Laura away after breakfast and went up to the main branch of the New York Public Library. There, I could be guaranteed a certain anonymity. It is a huge, cold place full of strangers. All kinds of people can come there with all kinds of schemes and never be detected. Maniac scholars sit in the reading room writing treatises on cosmic force and mumbling to themselves as girls go by in short skirts. Anarchists plan universal destruction. Aspiring young professors write dissertations and surreptitiously finger their shrinking genitals. It is a microcosm, a Babel, the ultimate proof that accumulated knowledge is a mad and pointless enterprise. I go there often to reassure myself that I have lost nothing by shunning the purely intellectual life.

This time, however, my mission was more specific. Armed with a few dimes and a rough outline, I composed my letter of application to Gertrude on one of the public typewriters. The letter was a masterpiece of tact·and seductiveness: 'I am a man of fifty-five in vigorous good health.' As I wrote, I rehearsed my new voice. It would be British and educated but not theatrically exaggerated. Perhaps Claude had spent some time in Canada, which might account for a slight Americanising of his speech. 'I was born in London, but have travelled widely. I made my living as a carpenter and attended evening classes at the University of London. I became interested in the theatre and took up playwriting, which I continue to this day, though I play only to an audience of one. After service in the R.A.F. in World War II, I took a position supervising the estate of J. Roger Higgins, M.P., near Chelmsford in Essex. I have from him letters of reference which I will be happy to submit should they be required. Three years ago, I emigrated to Canada, where I held a variety of positions. I have come now to America to start life anew. I am a bachelor and somewhat of a recluse by nature. I am fond of the country and do not mind hard work. I do not drink or smoke to excess and have no other vices. Should an interview be in order, please write to me at the above address.'

I left a blank where the address should have been. Ideally, I should have a real address, a small hotel or rooming house, to which I could be traced, and where I might, so to speak, establish my residence and get to be known. But this will take time and cannot be done until Claude Elmath is properly costumed and invested with the breath of life. I had no choice but to go to the Grand Central branch of the Post Office and take out a box. I used Claude's name, of course, which gave me an odd sense of pleasure and relief that I can't quite explain. I walked quickly back to the library and typed in the address. After ten minutes of practice, I developed a left-handed signature that seemed reasonably appropriate. It was a risk, of course, to put anything in writing with either hand, but I could think of no alternative and Gertrude might think it strange if the letter went unsigned. I weighed the advantages and disadvantages and decided to gamble.

My next problem was more difficult. I had to devise some kind of a make-shift disguise in order to approach the theatrical wig-maker who would fit me for hair and beard. For one thing, I could not risk being identified at some future time, should the police be even half as thorough as they are made to seem in detective novels. Secondly, I would have no logical explanation to offer the wig-maker, unless I was in some way connected with the theatre. I decided, therefore, to become an actor-director and to invent a suburban community theatre that sounded plausible, ordinary and obscure. I dismissed Westport, Greenwich, Westbury, Long Beach, Fort Lee, and settled on Tenafly, New Jersey. Perhaps because I had never been to Tenafly and, therefore, assumed, in some childish way, that no one else had ever been there either. I had no way of guessing where the wig-maker came from. It was possible that he knew Tenafly well. There was an outside chance that he even lived there and commuted to the city, but one must always play the odds. It seemed to me a sufficiently unlikely coincidence.

I don't know where I got the name John Dickey. I wanted an ordinary name, but nothing as obvious as John Smith. Dickey conjured up in my mind a little man surrounded by picket fences, insurance policies, chinless children, and bored middle-class neighbours, who might conceivably get together to put on a production of *Our Town* or *Macbeth*, if only to get away from their husbands or wives in order to indulge in a little surreptitious suburban sex. I thought of John Dickey as a commuting minor executive with Proctor and Gamble; a man approximately my own age, clean-shaven, and bespectacled, perhaps from birth.

In this role, I would place an order with Zappulla & Sons for one abundantly hairy King Lear. To transform myself into this depressing man from the suburbs I visited a while-u-wait optician on Third Avenue, where I explained that I seemed to be suffering from eye-strain. The optometrist on duty took me into a dark room, sat me in front of some antique machinery, asked me to read this and that, and within five minutes, confirmed the fact that I was, indeed, suffering from eye-strain. He referred me to his partner, a distracted little Jew, who tried to sell me everything but the inexpensive black frames that I selected. The lenses proved to be nothing but curved pieces of plain glass. It occurred to me later that they probably did a lot of business with people who wanted glasses for purely decorative purposes and that I really didn't have to go through the pretence and examination after all.

On my way back to the theatre district, I stopped in a drug store and bought a small jar of vaseline and some cottonwool. In the men's room in Grand Central Station, standing in a cubicle for which one pays a dime, I put on my glasses, slicked down my hair with vaseline, stuffed a little cottonwool in my mouth to bring out my cheeks and jowls and practised a slight slouch. I left the vaseline and cottonwool in the stall, amused by what the next customer might think.

Zappulla & Sons is an old theatrical wig and make-up establishment housed in an inconspicuous loft on West Forty-fifth Street.

Their ad in the *Yellow Pages* gave me the impression that they had been around a long time and were perhaps one of the best. I could not stint on my hair and beard. It had to be absolutely convincing, not only to Gertrude, but to that handful of people who would help to give Claude Elmath a real identity by swearing to the police that he existed.

Aldo Zappulla senior took care of me himself. He was a thick little Italian with a forehead like Il Duce and eyebrows that were perpetually raised over round eyes and deep shadows, as though the world was a constant amazement to him. He said that *King Lear* was a pretty ambitious play for a small community group. I agreed but offered no explanation. He asked me a second time what the name of the group was. I told him. He searched his memory and shook his head, repeating *Tenafly* several times, as though the fault was his for having an incomplete mental catalogue. I was relieved when he dropped the subject and turned his attention once again to the problem of transforming me into a raging old man. My plan was to order a grey wig and beard for Lear and then dye it back to middle-age, leaving a little grey at the temples, and trimming it to modern neatness. This might reduce the chances of detection should Claude's picture appear in the newspapers.

I had dinner at the Haleys' in Garden City, where I was exposed to some relatives. I met Virgil Haley, Laura's uncle, a man in his late forties or early fifties with an American Legion handshake and a rotundity that made it difficult for him to keep his pants up. I asked him if he knew who his famous namesake was. When he laughed, he looked like an old-fashioned Irish cop out of the movies. I was forced to explain about the Roman poet and Virgil Haley looked at me for a moment as though I were a communist or a homosexual. He was convinced that Virgil was a good old American name but out of deference to my newness in the family, did not argue the point too vigorously.

Virgil's wife, Helen (I dared not mention Troy lest it be mistaken for a city upstate), is a woman about forty with ridiculous red hair that could not have been the result of any normal combination of genes. Her face is appropriately ridiculous, a mask of plucked eyebrows, cosmetic-abused skin, and a lipsticked mouth more ambitious in its fullness than the mean slit that an ungenerous God endowed her with. Her one redeeming feature (assuming it is genuine) is a full bosom, which on essentially thin women is always rather interesting.

To complete this family portrait, there was a daughter, a wayward girl of sixteen, with the likely name of Eve. Laura had mentioned some of this girl's exploits and I had looked forward to meeting her. She was the only one in the family whose eyes betrayed any spark of intelligence. She could thank her mother for her generous chest, which she tried her best to display to the world. I found her quite charming, and, were the circumstances less confining, I might have tested her in some subtle way. As it is, I felt her breast against my arm as we selected records for the phonograph after dinner. I think it would not have been difficult to lure her into the basement or the backyard, where she could commit an act of rebellion against her ugly parents. For a while, I was quite distracted.

To this rather unpleasant family gathering, Gladys Haley contributed her mother and father, both about seventy years old, and her younger sister, a thirty-five year old divorcée with two terrible children. The message I received from Barbara Haley's glance did not need decoding. During the course of the evening, she trapped me in the corridor as I emerged from the bathroom. She said in conspiratorial tones, her hands all over me as though I were a child, 'I'm so glad you're joining the family. We need some new blood around here.'

Before the evening was over, I could tell that the big issue was my age. Everyone was very polite about it but it was clear that I was somewhat closer to the parental generation than to Laura's. The fact that Laura's little eighteen-year-old brother Ronnie was present did not help matters. Laura's mother is only forty-five and could easily be my sister. Grandpa Smith looked at me from time to time as though I were a molester of children.

It was a noisy evening, full of beer, pork and conversations about automobiles. Virgil Haley laughed explosively at jokes that might have been mistaken for obituary announcements.

Grandma Smith made squeaking noises about the depression to Barbara's two small boys when they fed stringbeans to the dog. And Ronnie, a freshman at Adelphi, played acid rock on his new cassette.

Laura was oddly unembarrassed by the whole thing and may even have imagined that I enjoyed being taken into the bosom of her family circle after a lonely life with Gertrude. It is, I must confess, a family with sufficient bosom, but I do not look forward to endless Sunday gatherings of this sort. I prefer to believe that I am kidnapping Laura into a more sophisticated and adventurous life, a life full of passion, art and natural beauty. There will be no noise in our Lloyd Harbor house. We will talk in whispers against the background music of birds or the crackling of the fire. God, how I hate stupidity, crudeness and noise!

After the visiting Haleys and Smiths were gone, I found myself alone in the living room with Gladys. Laura and her father had volunteered to do the dishes and young Ronnie had retreated to his masturbatorium on the second floor. We were sipping Christian Brothers brandy and smoking. We had an odd little conversation before we were interrupted. I think she was trying to find out whether or not I ever got laid. She was very roundabout, generalising in a matronly way about men. 'Your bachelor days are almost over,' she said. 'Are you sorry?' I smiled without answering. 'I imagine you've enjoyed a lot of freedom,' she said. I agreed non-committally. 'I mean a good-looking young man like you must have had some good times.' I said that good times didn't necessarily end with marriage. And before she could censor herself, she blurted out, 'That's what you think!' In that instant, her whole, ugly, frustrating marriage with Homer flashed before me. I could see her smoking intensely in the middle of the night, her snoring husband beside her in bed, smelling at both ends, bald and nearly impotent. Her hand moves into her crotch. Her thighs tighten. She is angry and ashamed but unless she does something she won't sleep.

Gladys reached over and touched my arm. 'If you're too tired to go home, you're welcome to stay over,' she said. It sounded like a proposition and I knew in that instant that, under the right circumstances, Gladys Haley could be had.

When I got back to my apartment, I was about to put the key in the door when I noticed that the door across the hall was ajar. New tenants had moved in recently, two young nurses from St. Vincent's. There was no light on in the apartment and there were no sounds. I felt my breathing increase. It was late. The hallway was quiet, an exciting no-man's land between my place and theirs. I turned the key softly and pushed open my door, but I did not go in. Instead, I went into the darkened apartment across the hall. I stood for a while in the living room, listening for signs of life. It was a small apartment with one bedroom. When my eyes became accustomed to the darkness, I could see that the two girls were asleep in twin beds. I stood trembling in the shadows, staring at the girl nearest me, whose sheet was drawn only up to her waist. She wore a flimsy nightgown, from which one large breast had almost totally escaped. I partially undid my clothes. For what purpose I did not at first know. I wanted desperately to touch the girl's breast, I was flushed, almost feverish with wild excitement. I inched towards her, my heart pounding so hard that I was afraid it would burst. I cupped my hand very lightly over her breast, feeling her nipple and the resiliency of her flesh. The blood rushing through my head made me dizzy and I was afraid I might black out again. As I retreated, she stirred lightly but did not wake up.

Back in my apartment, I locked the door and poured myself a generous Scotch. As I struggled with the icetray, I could see that my hands were trembling. It was a foolish thing I had done. It was the wrong time to be taking unnecessary risks. But at the moment when the incident occurred, I was oddly blind to the consequences. Nothing seemed to matter but going into that dark room like a thief and touching that sleeping girl. I cannot describe the intense excitement nor do I understand it. Something is happening to me. All my reactions are heightened. My perceptions are more profound. My skin is more sensitive. Perhaps there is too much adrenalin in my system.

Sunday, 18 May

After breakfast, I called up Laura to tell her what a wonderful time I had at her house last night and how much I liked her relatives. 'They thought you were great,' she said. 'They really liked you a lot.' I said I liked them a lot too, especially Uncle Virgil. 'Oh, he's a real character. But he's got a heart of gold.' Yeah, and a tin brain, I wanted to add but restrained myself. After a few more lies and some amorous noises, I hung up and got to work.

The first thing I had to do was to write Claude Elmath's 'autobiography'. I had to know him thoroughly. I had to invent a family for him, a boyhood and young manhood. I had to familiarise myself with his wartime experiences and those difficult post-war years when he was trying to 'find himself'. It took me fully two hours and half a pack of cigarettes to produce the following document :

'My father was Paul Elmath of Stratford. He came to London as a young man to make his fortune. There he set up as a cabinet-maker and rapidly earned a reputation as an excellent craftsman. Though he did not make a fortune, he made a good living. He married Elizabeth Turner in his thirtieth year and had four children, of whom I was the youngest. I have two older sisters Mary and Joyce—and an older brother who emigrated to Australia and disappeared mysteriously in the back country. The sisters are married and living in middle-class comfort in Swiss Cottage. They have produced for me a small army of nieces and nephews, from whom I hear only occasionally about marriages, deaths, and births.

'When I was a child, we lived in a house in Soho. There was always a great deal of noise in the house. I'm not sure why. Being the youngest, I felt I had to compete with my brother and sisters. The fact that they were able to do things that I could not do sometimes filled me with a sense of inadequacy. However, I was more secure in the affections of my mother and we became the greatest of friends. Her sudden death when I was only sixteen was a tragedy from which I may never recover. My father, too, felt the loss profoundly. Within two years, he was dead of what I always felt was a broken heart.

'My brother and I kept the shop open and made a fair living from it until he decided that there was greater promise in the land down under. I went on alone for a while but found the work dreary and dreaded repeating the quiet, pointless life my father had led. The house and the shop were sold and I went off into the world on my own. I took miscellaneous jobs as a carpenter and spent much of my spare time in the theatre. At first, I dreamed of acting as a career but soon shifted my attention to playwriting. I took courses at night at the University of London and I joined a community drama club.

'It was during a production of *Othello* that I met Maggie St. Clair. She was a tall lovely girl with blonde hair and blue eyes. I lost my heart to her instantly. And every time I saw that blackamoor, played by Reginald Stone, strangling her on the bed, it made me furious with jealousy. By the time I worked up enough courage to confess my profound affection, it was too late. There must have been something seductive in Reginald's brutality. Or else he was a bit more tender offstage. In any case, Reginald and Maggie were soon married. The wedding was held at the Brompton Theatre and we all drank champagne. I did a marvellous Pagliacci, weeping on the inside, but laughing on the outside, and went home after the party, planning to blow my brains out.

'Had I not lived so far from the theatre I might have carried out my plan. However, during the long walk home I reconsidered and decided, instead, to join the R.A.F. The war in Europe was brewing and I thought I might see some action. During the five years that followed, I saw more action than I bargained for and lost my taste for adventure. I was shot down over occupied Holland and spent six months with the Underground. The Germans were constantly searching for us and threatening death to those who protected us. In an attempt to cross the Rhine to the Allied lines, several of us were captured and spent the rest of the war in a POW camp.

'After the war, I was determined to be the modern Shakespeare. Adrift in Soho for a year or more, I scribbled in frigid furnished rooms and spent much time at the British Museum. But nothing came of my efforts and I soon grew weary of the bohemian life. I decided that what I needed was peace and quiet and the joys of nature. I went to work as the caretaker of the estate of J. Roger Higgins, M.P., near Chelmsford in Essex. Still secretly in love with Maggie St. Clair, I could not become intimate with any other woman. My friendly involvement with the inn-keeper's daughter can hardly be counted as a love affair.

'Time passed and I grew older. I continued to write my plays, but with less and less enthusiasm. I continued to frequent the little pub nearby, but also with less and less enthusiasm. I decided I was growing stale. It was time to move on. Canada seemed like a sufficient frontier and off I went with a few hundred pounds and high hopes for a new life in my middle age. But Canada proved a bore with its awful provincialism and its freezing winters. I worked as a carpenter in Toronto and as a lumberjack in British Columbia. I moved about continually and felt a growing restlessness and dissatisfaction. At last, I decided to try America, that great land of promise. And here I am on the brink of a new adventure, in good health, incurably optimistic, and one or two steps ahead of poverty. I have applied for a job as a caretaker for an estate on Long Island. Who knows what will come of it.'

I spent the rest of the day on my project. I was beginning to feel quite competent at this sort of thing. I had to call Zappulla to make sure the job would be done in time. I had to try out the disguise some way, perhaps shopping in familiar places. I had to call Gertrude Monday evening to see whether or not my letter of application had been received. I had to answer an ad in *The Village Voice* about a small second-hand printing press to take care of the stationery problem for letters of reference and other false documents. I had to find out exactly what Emma the maid's schedule was. She is there mostly mornings, I think. I must figure out a convenient way to carry the disguise and a convenient place where I can put it on. I must find a rooming house where I can live as Claude for a while prior to the murder. At all costs Claude must not be connected in any way with Marc McMann. He must not be seen coming out of this apartment. What weapons should I carry with me? If she cries out she must be killed immediately. If she recognises me she must also be killed immediately—unless I dismiss it all as an elaborate joke. But in that case the murder is off. I must check the doorman's schedule. I must get identification photos made as soon as the disguise is ready. Perhaps I should drug her tea.

At about six o'clock, just as I was building my Tower of Babel martini, as I call it, the phone rang. It was Jenny Hoffman announcing that our friend Paul Garrison had had a heart attack and was in St. Vincent's Hospital. I must have been speechless for longer than I imagined because Jenny kept saying, 'Hello, Marc, are you there?' Finally, I managed to say, 'Will he be all right?' My right hand clutched my left breast. I could feel my heart racing and I felt nauseous. She said it sounded like a mild attack but they did not know the extent of the damage as yet. She wasn't sure, but she thought he might have visitors. 'He was stricken last night at a party,' she said, and her choice of words brought back a thousand obituaries in which some poor son-of-a-bitch was *stricken* : at a party, at home, on the golf course, during the rehearsal of a play, after dinner, and oh Christ, in the subway. Imagine being *stricken* during a subway rush-hour. In his *Inferno*, Dante would have reserved such a punishment for regicides and homosexual popes. 'It might cheer him up to see a few people,' Jenny said. 'You know how Paul is.'

Hospitals are both depressing and exciting; depressing for the obvious reasons, and exciting because they provide the first glimpse into a future in which we will know all there is to know about the human body and be able to take it apart and put it together again and guarantee, if not immortality, then extremely long life. It makes me sick to think that I was born too soon. How ridiculous and unfair it will be if one day the problem of death is solved not in the church but in the laboratory. A million generations will have gone trembling to the universal gallows, to be followed by a species free from this fate. It's not fair. Damn it, it's not fair. I don't want to go down the drain as a primitive, a prelude to real human life. I want to be one of the new men. I want to live forever.

I went down a corridor, took an elevator, went down another corridor, apprehensive and eyeing the nursing nuns. I thought I could smell alcohol, ether, and clean linen. It was hospital smell.

Paul was in a private room in an oxygen tent. There was a large no-smoking sign because of the oxygen. He was sitting up nodding towards me and smiling feebly but it did not look like Paul; he looked like one of those mechanical fortune-tellers in the penny arcade. He was very pale. There was a tube connected to his arm, perhaps for intravenous feeding. I asked him how he felt but he could not hear too well through the plastic tent. I asked again and he nodded. I could tell he was scared. I could see it in his face.

It was awkward. I didn't know what to do or say. The bathroom door was open. I smiled, made idiot gestures and went in. I closed the door and quickly lit a cigarette. I took a deep drag and then another and dropped the thing into the toilet. It flushed quietly and I could see the cigarette go round and round two or three times before being sucked under.

When I came out again there was a priest in the room talking at the ghostly person in the oxygen tent who used to be Paul Garrison. I expected somebody to wheel in a coffin any minute. The priest, a youngish man, introduced himself as Father Frederick, an old friend of Paul's. 'It's not an official visit,' he said. The three-way conversation that followed was clumsy.

We said goodbye to Paul, who muttered something about having one for him, and went out together. In the dying daylight, the city seemed unreal. For a moment, I wanted to rush back into the hospital, where I could be placed in an oxygen tent and given intensive care by a whole convent of nuns. 'Can I buy you a drink?' said Father Frederick. His offer brought me back to reality and suddenly transformed him from a priest into an ordinary man.

We found a bar on Sixth Avenue and sat in a booth made of imitation red leather. 'We'll order three martinis,' said Father Frederick. 'One for Paul.' The waiter revealed nothing, neither puzzlement nor understanding. He merely brought the drinks and put them all in the centre of the table.

Father Frederick looked older in the dim light. I guessed that he might be as much as forty, but I really couldn't tell. We toasted Paul, touching his glass. 'I met Paul at a retreat a few years ago,' said Father Frederick. 'He wanted to come back to the Church.'

'I didn't know he was religious,' I said, feeling a bit foolish.

'Everybody's religious,' he said. 'We participate in the drama whether we like it or not. We are always either running towards God or away from Him.'

I saw myself galloping across a vast desert. Lawrence of Arabia. Jonas in the belly of the whale. I could not collect myself for a theological debate, but, oh, how I wanted to fling myself into the arms of this representative of the Mother Church. Jesus Saves! but Popoff picks his nose.

'You assume, of course, the existence of God,' I said

'You don't have to assume anything,' he said. 'The existence of God is as obvious as the existence of the world.' I looked again at Paul's martini glass. Nothing seemed obvious to me, unless it was the fact that we all die sooner or later. I said so and he laughed. He acted as though he had some secret knowledge. He was not unpleasant but I began to dislike him. I wanted to shout at him, 'How do you know? Just how the hell do you know what's going on, you arrogant son-of-a-bitch?' Instead I sipped at my drink and found it difficult to swallow. The air seemed suddenly thick and warm. I thought for a moment the drink would come up again and I swallowed hard.

He was talking in his calm voice about the leap of faith when a wave of panic came over me. I knew in that instant that I was going to die. It was not an idea, not a philosophical statement; it was an experience. I could feel it in my body. I could imagine my life oozing away. I could see the world the day after my death. I would be shoved out the door into the darkness and would never, never, never, never, never be able to come back. I would be dead. I would not exist any more. I saw my yellow, lifeless body being wheeled from Paul's hospital room to the morgue. I saw them cutting open my corpse to examine my diseases. I saw them lowering me into the earth and I remembered the mud in the driveway at Lloyd Harbor. I could feel it on my naked feet. I could hear the rain. From my bedroom window I could look towards the caretaker's cottage and beyond it to the water. I thought of Gertrude. Somehow her death didn't matter. Nobody's death mattered, only mine. Other people don't matter. Their death is not the same as my death. My death is personal. My desperate *self* is wrapped up with this disintegrating body, this dying animal. Oh Christ, what am I to do? What am I to do?

Father Frederick could see that something was wrong. He touched my arm. 'Are you all right?' he said. I told him I was feeling ill and had to leave. I tossed a crumpled dollar on the table and ran out of the bar before he could insist on coming with me. I walked quickly down Sixth and across Eleventh Street, swaying, not from the drink, which I barely touched, but from the pounding behind my eyes.

When I got home, I went immediately to bed, in spite of the fact that it was still very early. I pulled the covers up to my chin and stared at the pattern of shadows on the ceiling. I could feel my entire body tremble and my heart would not slow down. I wished at that moment that there was a God and that I could pray but even when I am most desperate, I know that there is no God and that it is pointless to pray. I waited for the mood to pass but I continued to be obsessed with death and putrefaction.

After a while, I fell asleep. I woke up about ten o'clock feeling disorientated and empty. I knew there were things I had to do, but I could not concentrate or generate any interest in them. I was in the grip of what Hemingway called 'black-ass'. I could feel myself slipping away—down, down. I was getting smaller and smaller. I was disappearing. There was only one real medicine for this mood. I needed a woman—or, more precisely, a woman's body. I needed the sex ritual, the seed-planting, the affirmation of Life in the face of Death. That's my religion. To hell with the Holy Ghost—give me the Good Goddess.

I hadn't planned to go to Julien Updike's party, but now I knew I had to. I was sure to find what I needed there.

Julien Updike is a professor of English and an unsuccessful novelist, a type as common as grass these days in the intellectual world. His wife Emma is lean, hungry and a reluctant forty. Needless to say, she paints. To ward off the Eternal Executioner, they have allied themselves with the new bohemianism, whatever its current name. They are fond of drugs, demonstrations, and group sex. As interior decorators, they are practically reactionaries, relying heavily on brick-and-board bookcases, mobiles and op-art.

Amidst saris, serapes and nervous faces, each talking or smiling inside a bubble of isolation, I stalked my prey, my little gazelle. A pretty girl. A thin, blonde, dreamy girl. Inarticulate. In touch with her mortal ancestors and her immortal creator. I sang to her —words, of course. I hypnotised her. I forced her to imagine that the thing we were about to do was inevitable and necessary. And then I led her away, her small arm fragile in my firm grip. The only private and lockable place I could find was the bathroom in the master bedroom. She stood like an obedient child as I undressed her. And then, since there was no room to lie down, I took her standing up, a difficult but not impossible position. I left her brushing her hair in front of the mirror, apparently unmoved by my attentions—at peace with herself and her mirror image. Which is more than I could say for myself. I made my way through the party-people towards the door. It seemed to me that they spoke many foreign languages and had black hoods over their heads.

Monday, 19 May

At the office this morning, I tried to apply myself to the important task of creating textbooks for the young vipers of the love generation but my concern for their futures at I.B.M. was easily overshadowed by my concern for my own future in Lloyd Harbor. I was disturbed by my 'autobiography'. There were too many periods in Claude's life that were glossed over. In fact, as I read it over, I found the whole thing sketchy and unconvincing. For one thing, it gave no real insight into the man himself. What did he think? What were his plays about? Who were his friends? When did he first grow his beard? And, good lord, what exactly did he do during all those years in Chelmsford? Unless I knew my man perfectly, my whole plan might collapse. One hesitation, one contradiction, might give it all away. In a frantic moment, I actually slipped a piece of paper into the typewriter and started to write a play. If I had in hand a real manuscript then surely the world would believe that Claude Elmath really existed. He would never be traced to me. But an original manuscript, however bad, is not easy to produce. I considered Claude's background and experience. It is always best to write from experience. Perhaps, I thought, I should write about 'my' adventures in the war. A scene came to mind (had I stolen it from an old movie?) : There is a farmhouse in winter in Holland. The wind is howling outside. A family of frightened peasants is gathered around the meagre fire. There is a man of fifty, his plain wife, his beautiful daughter, and his shrivelled but wise old mother. There is a knock at the door. Everyone looks terrified. The farmer slowly slides back the bolt and opens the door. Another peasant is there. He is supporting a wounded airman. 'I found him in the woods,' he says. 'He has been three days without food and he is badly hurt.' The father of the family shakes his head. 'No, no, it is impossible,' he says. 'The Germans are in the village. They will kill us all if they find out. I have seen their patrols. They must know that a plane is down.' The argument goes on. The peasant at the door is a member of the Underground. 'Where is your humanity?' he says. 'Can you throw him out to die like a dog in the snow?' The farmer's beautiful daughter looks tenderly at the fallen bird of an airman. Three generations of women glance at one another and then at the frightened farmer. 'You heard what they did at Alderberg,' he says. There is a long silence as everyone considers Alderberg . . .

I went on that way for half an hour, not writing so much as merely day-dreaming the play. The whole thing was so pathetically awful that it might be convincing. Though I do not mean him to be unintelligent, Claude is, after all, an unsuccessful playwright. But when will I ever find time to do it.

I returned to Claude's Chelmsford days. He was already bearded. I saw him smoking a pipe. He wore a cap and a sagging tweed jacket with leather patches at the elbows. In the pub, he had his daily pint or two and threw darts with the other men. They could not have known him as he really was—a sensitive man, a wise man, a subverted artist, a man accustomed to loneliness but desperate for the affections of a good woman.

I went to the men's room, my mind still three thousand miles from the rattle of typewriters and the cold white urinal into which I stared. Hinkle came in and stood beside me. I looked at him blankly. 'How's it going?' he said, undoing his pants. His sudden appearance short-circuited the signal from my brain to my bladder and I stood there longer then I usually would, trying to re-establish communications. I grunted something incoherent to him and he smiled at me as his strong, efficient stream gurgled in the drain of the urinal. The son-of-a-bitch was showing off, I thought, and I felt like a failure, waiting for something to happen. After another moment or two of concentration, a weak dribble appeared. By this time, Hinkle was shaking himself vigorously, exhibiting all the confidence of an Olympic champion. 'Where are you going on your honeymoon?' he said. And an arrow of rage punctured my throat. 'None of your bloody business!' I said, struggling with my zipper. 'All right, all right,' he said. I caught a glimpse of his thing out of the corner of my eye. It was much larger than I had imagined or hoped it would be.

I met Laura for lunch at Gino's Kitchen, a cheap Italian restaurant halfway between her office and mine. From the moment she walked in, I could tell that something was bothering her. Laura is not accustomed to having complicated thoughts, and is, therefore, not very good at concealing them. On the lovely terrain of her face, a problem will appear like an ugly billboard peddling unhappiness, 'What's wrong, baby?' I said, studying her across the small table. 'Oh nothing, nothing at all,' she said. 'I just didn't sleep very well last night.'

Since Laura is the sort of girl who might easily sleep through World War III, I was more convinced than ever that something was going on. She tried to change the subject, using a brave little voice to talk about a boring lawsuit on which her boss was working. But she was only a few minutes into her feeble camouflage when her lower lip began to quiver and her usually clear eyes misted over. She blinked rapidly and looked into her glass of wine. 'Come on, baby, tell me what it is,' I said, touching her hand.

'Oh, it's nothing, really,' she said. 'It's just Uncle Virgil. He came over last night to talk to Daddy. They were down in the den for about an hour, drinking beer and talking. Then they came up to the kitchen looking very serious. Mom and I were there making chocolate chip cookies. We had tea at the kitchen table and Daddy began to ask me peculiar questions.'

My heart contracted and I could feel my animal eyes narrow. 'What sort of questions?' I said.

'He wanted to know how well I really knew you, and what you've been doing all these years,' she said. 'He wanted to know why your mother was against the marriage and why you were thirty-five years old and not married yet. And he kept asking me if I was sure I knew what I was doing. All this time Uncle Virgil just sat there looking at me, as though I was a little girl or maybe a patient in a hospital or something. I told them that your mother had some strange ideas and that she sort of wanted to keep you all to herself because you're her only child. But I told them I was really sure I wanted to marry you. They kept on that way for a while and I guess I got upset. Mom got upset too. She hollered at them and said they were getting me all confused with all their mystery. "If there's anything you have to say, say it," she said. "Well, it's nothing very definite," Uncle Virgil said. "It's just that there's something funny-looking about that guy. I can't say exactly what it is, but something not right. Oh, he's handsome and smart all right. Still, he makes me wonder." Then he told us about this boy that he knew when he was in the navy in the war. He didn't say much about him, except that he was also handsome and smart, and that the other men laughed at him and took advantage of him. Daddy kept nodding as if he understood Uncle Virgil, but I didn't know what he was trying to say and, after a while, I began to cry and I went up to my room. Mom came up and said, "Don't listen to those idiots. They don't know what they're talking about." I didn't want to talk about it any more, so I went to bed.'

'Is that all?' I said, controlling my fury. In my personal torture chamber, I had Uncle Virgil chained to the wall and I was burning out his eyes with a hot iron, after which I would remove his testicles and stuff them in his fat mouth.

'That's all,' she said. 'I know I was foolish to let them upset me, but I honestly didn't know what to think.'

I forced a smile and tightened my grip on her hand. 'Well, don't worry about it, sweetheart,' I said 'Your Uncle Virgil probably means well, but he has some peculiar ideas.'

'I don't understand,' she said. 'What was he trying to tell me?'

'He thinks that unless a man is fat and full of tattoos he's not really a man.'

A slow dawn of realisation spread over Laura's face. 'Oh,' she said, 'is *that* what he was trying to say? Now isn't that ridiculous? Of course, you're a real man. I mean if anybody ought to know, I ought to.' Her smile lingered for a few minutes and we bathed in the sunlight of reassurance. But just before we were interrupted by the waiter I saw her frown for a second, as though she were remembering something unpleasant.

After lunch, I called the office to tell them that I would be spending the afternoon at the library doing research. This dodge is to editors what periodic cramps are to secretaries. I called about the printing press that was advertised in *The Village Voice* and spoke to someone with a weak monotone who might have been male or female, old or young, dead or alive. The voice said, 'Like any time is all right,' and directed me to an apartment on Thompson Street.

There is something sexually exciting about cool, dark hallways in tenement buildings. Perhaps it's the idea that behind each door there are naked people doing private things. Sometimes, I am tempted to knock at the wrong door in the hope of surprising a lonely housewife in a state of undress. Some of them are certainly waiting for the unexpected adventure. I know, because I myself have waited restlessly in my own apartment, hoping that someone would appear—a beautiful stranger.

I knocked gently and waited. I heard footsteps and then the click of a lock. The door opened and I saw in the dim light the ghost of D. H. Lawrence. When he spoke, I knew I was in the right place. He led me through the kitchen into a cluttered living room. There was a bathtub in the kitchen, and a toilet without a door. The table was piled high with dirty dishes and newspapers. The floor was bare. In the living room, there was a girl in an open red vest nursing a baby. She looked like an Indian squaw, except that her hair was blonde and quite long. She came out of her trance for a moment and glanced at me and then went back to her romance with her infant. Her breasts were swollen with milk, and the nipples were reddish-brown and erect.

'We were putting out a little magazine called *Nada*,' said the hungry-looking young man, 'but we ran out of bread.'

'What kind of a magazine was it?' I said.

'It was a magazine of anarchist aesthetics,' he said. He pulled aside a dirty sheet to reveal the press. It was smaller than I imagined it would be. It looked, in fact, like a toy.

'What do you mean by anarchist aesthetics?' I said.

A laugh escaped from his unsmiling face, as though it were

dubbed in. 'The artist as destroyer,' he said. 'The illusion of form shattered.' He stooped over to lift the press into the centre of the room and my eyes wandered to the half-naked girl. She was rocking gently back and forth, as though keeping time to secret music. 'There's enough type here to set a page of prose,' he said. He turned suddenly and caught me looking at the girl. 'Isn't that beautiful?' he said. I nodded, a little embarrassed. He went to the girl and touched her hair. She did not look up from her erotic work. 'I call her the stoned madonna,' he said. His hand wandered down to her shoulder and then to her breast. 'Her milk is stronger than Moroccan hash.' He bent over and took her nipple in his mouth and made a sucking noise for a minute and then stood up. He laughed again behind his beard and returned to the press. The girl never moved or seemed aware of my existence.

'You can have the whole thing for fifty bucks,' he said. For a moment I thought he meant apartment, bathtub, girl, and everything. 'We've got to split now and it's a real drag.'

I looked blankly at the press and at the founts of type. 'All right,' I said.

I paid him in cash and he helped me carry the thing downstairs, where I had to wait fifteen minutes before a taxi came by.

After the seven o'clock news, I called Gertrude. It was hard to determine what her mood was without seeing her. She was unusually talkative, which might be either elation or tension. 'I had lunch today with Charlie Davidson,' she said, and I straightened up as though I had been punched in the kidneys. Davidson is her lawyer.

'What was the occasion?' I said.

'Oh, mostly business,' she said, secretive and ambiguous as usual. I was tempted to ask directly about her will but I couldn't quite bring myself to it. 'Charlie was in rare form. I've never seen him look better. He talked me into having a drink before lunch. Now, you know I never drink during the day, and in fact, hardly drink at all. Well, that one whisky sour went right to my head and half the time I wasn't quite sure what I was saying.

There are some tax problems apparently. But I won't bore you with business. Besides, I don't really understand it myself—all those stocks and bonds, capital gains, and inheritance taxes.'

Once more I felt the fist in the kidneys and I began to suspect that Gertrude was fighting dirty. Surely she knew what she was doing. I danced away from her and threw a few fast jabs. 'I thought I might drive out to Lloyd Harbor sometime and show Laura the house,' I said. 'Would you mind?'

'Right now the place is a bit of a mess,' she said. 'Especially the grounds.'

She blocked my left, but I came back with a hard right. 'By the way,' I said, 'did you get any answers to your ad in the *Times*?'

There was a pause and my heart responded with a momentary hesitation. Why didn't she answer right away? I could hear her breathing. I imagined it was a long time before she said anything. Actually, it might only have been a second or two. 'I had two replies,' she said.

I had to coax her. 'Were they any good?' I said.

'As a matter of fact,' she said, 'both of them sound excellent.' Once again she hesitated. What the hell was the matter, I wondered. Did she suspect something already? Or was it just the old secretiveness again.

I should have dropped it right there, but I had to go a step further, I had to find out whether or not she was referring to Claude Elmath. I didn't know how to phrase the next question, and without thinking I blurted out, 'What nationalities are they?'

'What an odd question,' she said. 'What makes you think they're not Americans?'

Sheer genius rescued me. 'I was thinking of the caretakers at the Dalton house. They were a Swedish couple, weren't they?'

'Well, neither of these men is Swedish,' she said, somewhat annoyed at having been driven out into the open. 'One is from Pennsylvania and the other is English.'

Without knowing anything about him, I was suddenly violently jealous of this man from Pennsylvania. What business did he have applying to be my mother's caretaker? I wanted to kill him. 'Where in Pennsylvania?' I said.

'Oh, he's living in the city right now,' she said. 'He used to work on the country estate of some writer who died. I forget his name.'

'And the other man?' I said.

'He sounds fine. He's had a lot of experience, but mostly in England. I won't be able to tell anything really, though, until I see them in person.'

That was all I wanted to hear. I was violently excited and practically hung up on her. I wanted to get back to work.

I spent the next few hours playing with the press. I've always had a kind of passion for the printed word. My first effort was surprisingly good, perhaps not exactly what J. Roger Higgins himself would have chosen, but more than adequate for my purposes. Obviously, I have a real genius for this kind of work.

At eleven o'clock, I watched the news again on television. It was essentially the same news that I watched at seven, but it didn't matter.

Tuesday, 20 May

I sometimes practise being old. I wake up in the morning, astounded to be alive still. I lie in bed and imagine that I am seventy-five years old. My face is wrinkled and I am toothless. I watch the first light of the dawn creep across the sky. I have an eerie, end-of-the-world feeling. Everybody is dead, except me. All those children in the sixth grade, whom I remember vividly, are now, one way or another, broken by time, rotted out. Little Mary O'Neil, all peaches and pigtails, is now an antique hag with internal bleeding and flaps of yellow skin for breasts. How I loved her before time intruded. I think of Claudio in *Measure for Measure* : 'If I must die, I will encounter darkness as a bride, and hug it in mine arms.'

I was enormously agitated all day. Even the stelazine didn't seem to help much. I had a strong impulse to masturbate under my desk while Linda was sitting there taking dictation. It took me a long time to compose a very short letter. I folded my arms across my chest, not only to control my hands, but also to feel the pounding of my heart. I have always assumed that if I could actually feel my heart beating, it couldn't possibly stop.

I was excited not only by Linda's generous bosom, but by the sight of almost any woman under sixty. I left my cubicle door open and watched the girls go back and forth. I took the elevator to the top floor and then wandered down five floors to my own level stopping briefly here and there to look at the girls. The building was full of them and most of them were young. A few nodded hello; others looked at me blankly, as though they were not sure they had ever seen me before. In the book-keeping department, I lingered by the water cooler, from which I could see a girl named Dolores. She had very long legs and a thin waist and could not have been over nineteen. Her grace and beauty were mumbled about in men's rooms throughout the building. On first encountering her, one might easily imagine her an earth-bound angel but the moment she opened her mouth she disqualified herself from celestial considerations. There could be no doubt about her grubby origins in the South Bronx, nor about her dismal future as the wife of an alcoholic bricklayer.

Having made the grand tour, I returned to my desk and forced myself to read through my correspondence with Professor Leonard Kleinman. Shortly before noon, I called Zappulla & Sons to make absolutely sure my hair and wig would be ready. I was told that I could pick them up any time between three and six. My heart fluttered and the rhythm of my breathing was interrupted for a moment. After I hung up, there was still a buzzing in my ear, an echo of the faulty connection.

I did not know I was going to Uncle Phil's apartment until I was almost there. But by the time I was rising in the slow antique elevator, I knew what it was that I wanted. I felt intuitively that Cousin Emily played an important part in my drama. Something about her aroused not only my curiosity but also my lust. Even her childish manner and her inability to speak excited me.

She opened the door and looked surprised. She was wearing a white blouse and white skirt, but no shoes. Her lips were painted cherry-red, but the lipstick was badly applied, as though she were a little girl playing at being a grown-up. Her brown hair was heaped on top of her head and held there with numerous hairpins. It looked ridiculous, though it heightened the delicate elegance of her features. I wondered what she did all day in that empty apartment.

She seemed happy to see me and indicated a chair as an invitation to sit down. 'Do you have any Scotch?' I said, and she produced a bottle and a glass. 'How about you?' I said, and she shook her head. She sat down on the hassock, almost at my feet, and stared at me. 'Is Uncle Phil here?' I said. She shook her head.

I tried a series of questions to which she might answer with a yes or no. Do you ever go out? Do you read a lot? Does my mother ever come to visit? Do you want to learn how to speak again? Does your father ever talk about the past? Does he treat you well? Does he have a lot of money? Do you like my mother? Do you ever want to get married?

At the last question she lowered her head and said quite clearly, 'Yes.' I was so astounded I stood up suddenly upsetting my glass. Then I was furious. I dragged her to her feet and held her by the arms. As I shook her the heaped arrangement of hair fell apart.

'You can talk,' I said angrily. 'Well, then, damn it, why the big silent act?'

Her smile was both pathetic and sinister, but she did not say anything. Her eyes drifted back to mine and stared defiantly.

I shook her again. 'Well, come on, speak up,' I said.

She tried to pull away. I tightened my hold on her and drew her towards me. Her silence, which I had so admired, was suddenly offensive, a kind of insult, or even a weapon. I hugged her to me, but not amorously. 'Tell me what's going on, damn you,' I said. But with a burst of energy she tore away from me and fled towards her bedroom. I caught the door before it slammed and forced my way in. She backed off towards the bed. 'Don't be afraid,' I said. 'I'm not going to hurt you. I just want to know what's going on. Why don't you speak? Does it have anything to do with your father?'

She didn't answer. She backed into a sitting position on her bed and picked up the teddy bear and hugged him as though for protection. That annoyed me even more. I pulled the toy away from her and flung it across the room. She leapt up and slapped me hard across the face. Instinctively I responded in kind, leaving an irregular blush on her left cheek. A half-suppressed shriek escaped from her and she threw herself at me. I crushed her against my chest to immobilise her. She fought back and her squirming body excited me. I reached behind her and tore away her blouse. Then I allowed her to back away. She eyed me cautiously like a frightened animal. I too was an animal, and in my excitement I could not remember why I was attacking her.

Once again she was on the bed. I stood over her and ripped off the rest of her clothes. She winced at the ripping sound, as though it was her flesh that was being torn. But gradually her expression began to change, as though she were recovering her courage. By the time I removed her last garment, she was no longer struggling. But I was disappointed. I wanted her to struggle. I wanted to beat her. I wanted to take her by force. For a moment, I had an impulse to strangle her.

She lay there passively while I quickly undressed, her smile returning to remind me that she must certainly be containing a great secret. I knelt between her legs, my body poised above hers with straightened arms. We stared at each other for a long moment, my heavy breath too loud in the small room. At last her hand wandered to my shoulder and back. Before I knew what she was doing, her nails burned into my flesh. I plunged forward. Shivering and moaning, she arched towards me.

In a moment I was empty, body and mind, except for the lingering fear that now I must die. I had serviced the black widow and she had inflicted her fatal wound. Only life would go on. Only life, galloping recklessly into some dark future, thoughtless, directionless, ruthless.

It was almost three-thirty when I got back to work and I was late for a meeting in Mr. Pike's office. I felt dishevelled and self-conscious. I could feel the dampness under my shirt where Emily had wounded me. It forced me to think about her. I had uncovered one of her secrets, but not the other.

I moved with exaggerated caution, across the office to the one empty chair. No one even looked at me. Is it possible that I am invisible or that I do not exist at all?

I left the office at four-thirty and went uptown to pick up my hair and beard at Zappulla & Sons. Once again I transformed myself into that man from Tenafly with vaseline and cotton-wool, which was not difficult in the underground city around Thirty-fourth Street. Aldo Zappulla greeted me as though I were an old friend. 'And how is the big production going?' he said. I told him that everything was fine and that I was in a hurry to get home for dinner. He asked me again what the name of our group was but I could not remember what I told him the first time, so I said it was just a small community group. He stopped talking and before long made me over into a raging old man.

But Claude Elmath is not King Lear. Claude is younger, more sensible, more even-tempered, one in whom blood and judgment are well co-mingled. One who is cool under fire, a potential hero but a modest man. And his modesty is part of his charm, because he is, above all, charming.

I thought of these things in the taxi on my way home, trying to fill out my character. At home I set to work trimming and dyeing the hair and beard of my 'walking shadow'. There had to be enough grey to suggest the settled reliability of middle age, but enough black to indicate lingering youthfulness and virility.

As I worked, I tried to complete the portrait of Claude. I had a feeling that much was missing, that perhaps I was being abstract. I forced myself to be more specific. What, for instance, I asked myself, was Claude's favourite meat? What about fish? I decided that he'd like red snapper. But then it occurred to me that red snapper might not be available in England, or that if it were, perhaps the English call it something else. I shifted to cod. It was much simpler. Among the vegetables I decided that potatoes were out. I think of Claude as lean and hard, with none of that lower-class workman's accumulation of fat that can be attributed mainly to potatoes and beer. He would be, I decided, extremely fond of artichokes but he would settle, on ordinary occasions, for spinach, creamed onions, or beets.

What else? What else? Does he wear any rings? Yes. No. Yes, he wears a ring on the little finger of his left hand. No, that's ridiculous. He's not the Mississippi gambler; he's an honest, straight-forward man. No rings, no decorations. Steel-blue eyes and a firm hand. He drinks his whisky neat. What else? What else? What about his medical history? I would like to give him malaria, but his service was in Europe, not in Africa. And think of the possibilities of polio or a fall from a horse : crippled in childhood, destined never to walk again, Claude, by sheer will and determination, does the impossible. Not only does he not die; not only does he walk again, but by the time he is a boy of seventeen, he wins the cross-country title for his school and the highly coveted Bingley-Bowen trophy. But that would mean re-writing my autobiography. It's too complicated. I will make him chronically healthy, though it may diminish his glamour a bit.

What else? What else? Are his teeth his own? Does he have receding gums? Does he have any peculiar habits? Idiosyncrasies? Yes, he tends to stuff his pipe with the forefinger of his right hand, on which I might arrange a yellow stain. Perhaps he drinks hot water and lemon in the morning, instead of tea, though it seems unlikely. He must have a perfect digestive system. There is nothing more disturbing to a woman than to be reminded that men come completely equipped with the vulgar organs of animals. They like to feed them and imagine that the food is totally absorbed and never heard from again.

What else? What else? Good lord, how much there is to a man's life, how many thousands of bits and pieces. And yet with a thump or a sigh he can fall so easily into oblivion. What shall I say if she asks me about transplanting peonies? I must buy a book on gardening.

It took me almost two hours to get exactly the effect that I wanted. Then I stood before the mirror and tried on Claude Elmath. It was a terrifying and exciting experience to see myself transformed.

I stared for a long time at the bearded man in the mirror. He stared back at me with a curious and slightly amused look on his face. Everything fitted perfectly and seemed, at least under these circumstances, absolutely convincing. My face took on a more placid and serious look. I saw lines around my eyes that I had not noticed before. In an instant, I had aged twenty years. I marvelled at the scientific advancements that made my make-up possible.

I could not resist the temptation to try my disguise in public. As soon as it was dark, I went out, Claude Elmath stuffed into the pocket of my blazer. In the men's room of a subway station, I made the change. I was eager to walk the street, to show myself to the world, to talk, to breathe, to live as Claude Elmath. As

I emerged from the subway, I felt self-conscious. I also felt oddly stiff-jointed, as though I had been asleep for a long time.

My new identity gave me a sense of power. I asked a policeman for directions and almost exploded with sinister delight. I chatted with a cab driver and overtipped him. I bought some tobacco, weighed myself on a penny scale in a drugstore, and had a cup of coffee. Everything was new; everything was exciting. I was a fifty-five-year-old infant discovering the world for the first time.

In a cheap souvenir shop full of whirling tin gadgets, stuffed animals, and two-dollar cameras, I found one of those cubicles in which one can photograph oneself. With a greasy green curtain behind you, you sit and stare at a certain spot. The light goes on. There is a series of clicks and some buzzing sounds. You have the feeling that you're being watched. It's claustrophobic, coffin-like. And then you wait while automatic things happen in the ageing guts of the helplessly conditioned machine. After what seems like a small eternity of constipation, the creature produces a strip of four faces that vaguely resemble your own.

I grabbed the strip and studied the four poses of Claude Elmath. There he was smiling. There he was frowning, almost angry. In the third he might have been posing for the dust jacket of his new novel, and in the fourth he had a frightened look. For the first time that evening, somewhere beyond Claude, I could see myself.

I had come home as Marc, but as soon as I was safely locked in my apartment, I put on the disguise and once again studied myself in the mirror. My heart skipped. What about clothing? Did I dare wear my own clothing? How many crimes had been solved because the victim, clutching at the sleeve of her attacker, managed to pull away a few significant threads?

I took out my tape-recorder, ironically a gift from my mother, and practised my new voice and accent. It's very strange to talk out loud in an empty room. It's even stranger to speak in a voice that's not your own. But with practice the oddness wore off and I soon became quite accustomed to the new way of speaking. I read aloud from Shaw and Shakespeare and Oscar Wilde. I read *The Ballad of Reading Gaol*.

Wednesday, 21 May

At lunch, Laura leaned forward in her lux-bright innocence and said, 'What's wrong, Marc, you look funny?' I could not think of what to say at first, so I reached across and tenderly took her hand. With soap-box opera slowness I touched her fingers, expecially the one that bore my engagement ring. I looked into her face and then beyond her into the distance, as though I were seeing us in my mind sitting in front of a fire on our fiftieth wedding anniversary. Finally, I said, 'I don't want you ever to grow old.' It was a dumb thing to say and I don't quite know why I said it, but it worked. It was all the explanation Laura needed.

After lunch, I walked six blocks to the post office. I could see that there was something in my box and with trembling hands I struggled with the combination. At last, the little door came open and I took out a pale blue envelope. I recognised Gertrude's precise, feminine handwriting. 'Your qualifications for the position I have in mind seem quite good,' she wrote. 'I would welcome the opportunity to discuss the matter further with you. Would you be good enough to call me at the following number, so that we might arrange for an interview.'

I rushed home and got into bed. My head throbbed and I was flushed as though I had a fever but the rest of my body was abnormally cold. I took two tranquillisers and smoked a cigarette. Before long, the odd feeling subsided. I called the office and said that I would not be back. I explained to Linda that I thought I was coming down with something and was going to take it easy. 'Gee, that's too bad,' she said automatically. It was clear she didn't believe me. 'What do you want me to tell Hinkle?'

'Tell him I've got the bubonic plague,' I said.

'The what?' she said, as though I had been speaking Swahili.

'Never mind,' I said. 'Just tell him I'm sick.'

I don't know why I feel I have to get into bed when I am attacked by these moments of panic. Perhaps it's because I feel I'm going to die and it seems appropriate to die in bed.

After a while, I got up with renewed courage and calm to confront the situation. If I was going to go through with the whole scheme, then I had to work fast.

I took a chance and left my apartment as Claude Elmath. In the middle of the afternoon it was not likely that anyone would notice. However, I do not think I will risk it again. I took a taxi to Thirty-fourth Street where I bought a suitcase in Macy's. In another department I bought a pair of pyjamas, socks, underwear, shoes, two shirts, a tie, and a summer suit. It was not English, but it would have to do.

Back into the subterranean world I plunged, into the rumbling tunnels and stale air. I was Orpheus, I was Dante, I was the phoenix rising from its own ashes. In my rented cubicle, perfumed by urine and disinfectant, I put on my new clothes and stuffed the old ones into the suitcase. When I emerged I felt fresh and clean. But to be so thoroughly someone else was strange. I felt as though I were carrying my own corpse in that suitcase.

Once again I consulted the *Yellow Pages*. What a handy reference work for criminals! Without knowing anything about it I selected a place called the Saxon Arms Hotel. It sounded sufficiently respectable and inexpensive and was located on the West Side near the theatre district.

It proved to have all the dignity of an ageing prostitute. Its rugs were worn. Its chandeliers were antique. Though one could not see it, one had a sense of dust everywhere. It had a small lobby with deep maroon and brown leather chairs. The leather was real, but it was split here and there, and the wounds, like bleeding in reverse, revealed a flesh-coloured stuffing. Behind the carved reception desk was a skeleton of a man, whose skinny neck grew from his overly large collar like the stem of a plant. The stem flowered into gauntness and grey hair. His face was ravaged by time (most of the flesh was gone), but it was also collected, determined, and calm, as though he had started off a hundred years ago to run round the world and was just now coming to the finish line. I wondered how a man so weathered by experience could be deceived by anything. But then I consoled myself with the thought that he was probably as indifferent as he was wise.

'I would like a room with a bath,' I said in my rehearsed accent.

'For how long?' he said, absorbing me with his watery blue old eyes.

'I'm not sure,' I said. 'Perhaps a week, perhaps more.'

He made a clicking noise with his false teeth and pushed a card towards me. I signed with my left hand and Claude Elmath had a home. It was a small room full of two single beds and a large radiator. The ceiling was high and the walls were a dull green. Two slats in the venetian blind were missing but otherwise it seemed clean and adequate. There was even a tub in the bathroom, which was almost as large as the room itself.

I turned to tip the clerk but he had vanished, as though in that instant he had made the final leap from skeleton to ghost. I threw my suitcase on the bed and checked myself in the mirror. There I was. A man, one Claude Elmath, alone in a box of a room in the middle of New York City on a Wednesday afternoon. How convincing! How authentic!

I lit my pipe and went down to the lobby. I found the old desk clerk resurrected and well and quite talkative. His name was Chester, I discovered, and within fifteen minutes or so I learned that he had been many things in his long life before he descended to this humble post. He had been an inventor, contractor, gold prospector, stock speculator, salesman, sailor, golf pro, gambler, fruit-picker, and caretaker. I asked him, naturally, about his caretaking career. He said it was on Cape Cod and it consisted mostly of gardening and fishing and repairing the shutters. I don't know what I expected. Had there been an amorous side to his job he would hardly have mentioned it on such short acquaintance. In fact, at his age, he might even have forgotten what *amor* was. He said in the fall he would be eighty. Our conversation wore thin and his mouth made a wet clicking sound as though he was trying to taste something. I asked him if there was a bar in the hotel. He said no, but recommended the one immediately next door. 'Everybody goes there,' he said. I don't know who he meant by 'everybody,' but I nodded my thanks and went out.

The bar is called Sammy's. It's small and old and congenial, with lots of woodwork and tile floors. There are some high-backed booths but I chose a stool instead. I sat between a red-faced man who was gobbling peanuts and a middle-aged blonde who seemed to be dreaming of better days. I ordered a martini.

My efforts at communication were not generously rewarded. The red-faced peanut man was obsessed with baseball, and like all religious fanatics, he assumed that everyone knew what he was talking about. I interrupted his liturgy of batting averages to remind him that I was English and that we didn't have baseball in England. He looked at me suddenly as though I were a fly in his soup. 'Is that right?' he said, and allowed his attention to drift back towards the television set in the rear of the bar.

The woman, whose name was Nancy McGuire, was more agreeable. She had been living at the Saxon Arms for three years and said I could have it. I said no thanks and bought her a drink. Her tongue, which was already loose, began to grow thick. And the thicker it got the more she relied on the simple language of the street. 'These bastards are not looking for talent; they're looking for names,' she said. Which bastards exactly she was referring to I don't know. 'They string you along for a piece of ass and then they drop you. Well, you know what I say? I say piss on 'em.' She was sufficiently vulgar to be almost attractive, in spite of her forty-plus years. I thought of taking her to her room and hearing out the story of her dreary life between the sheets of a warm bed but it was apparent that as soon as she was horizontal poor Nancy would be asleep. Another time, I told myself, and escaped into the dying light of the early evening.

I went back to my room and for a while had the lost feeling that one has in hotel rooms. I didn't quite know what to do. I walked back and forth in the tight space. I looked out the window. I went to the bathroom and I opened my suitcase, as though it was necessary to unpack, and stared down at the empty, crumpled garments. How pathetic they were without Marc to fill them out. I shut the lid, as though it were the lid of a coffin, and lit a cigarette. After two puffs, I put it out and lit my pipe.

I sat on the bed for a long time re-reading Gertrude's letter to Claude and glancing at the phone. My heart began to beat faster as I rehearsed the call. I could feel my hands sweating and it was soon difficult to breathe. I sucked so nervously at the pipe that my tongue began to burn and a thin haze of smoke filled the room.

I was brief and to the point. I tried to avoid breathing too heavily into the mouthpiece. When I identified myself, she said, 'Oh, yes, when can you come for an interview?' I hesitated and cleared my throat. 'At your convenience, Mrs. McMann,' I said. 'How about tomorrow?' she said. Tomorrow? Good lord, so soon, I thought, but all I could say was, 'Yes, but after one,' keeping in mind the maid's schedule. We agreed on three o'clock and she hung up.

The tension subsided at first, but then began to mount again as I felt the impact of reality. I kept thinking, it's really going to happen. I'm going to do it. I'm really going to do it. I'm going to do it. Incredible! How utterly incredible! Then suddenly I was overwhelmed with hunger. If I didn't eat, I thought I might faint.

I went to the nearest restaurant and had red snapper with spinach and creamed onions. They did not have artichokes. I changed in the subway en route to my apartment and was home in time for the eleven o'clock news. I watched it blankly with a generous glass of Scotch in my hand and reviewed the events of the day.

At about midnight, I heard the elevator come up. I heard footsteps come down the hall but I did not hear a door open. I could sense someone directly outside. For a moment I thought it might be Gertrude, a kind of premature ghost come to haunt me. I listened again and then put on the safety chain and opened the door. I found one of the nurses fumbling in her bag in the dull light. 'Hello,' I said, 'anything wrong?' She gave me a buxom Irish smile. I love the way nurses' breasts bulge in their white uniforms. 'I don't seem to have my key and Mary's already asleep,' she said. 'Oh, that's too bad,' I said. 'Would you like to have another look in a better light?' She came in and looked again. The rest was easy. Her resistance was token and soon we were sweating and naked in bed, making the 'two-headed beast'. Once again, I had that awful insatiable feeling, the feeling that I had to do it and do it and do it until I fell down dead, because I couldn't get clear, couldn't swing free of the awful itch. What's wrong with me anyway? My fleshy young nurse, however, was delighted. By two o'clock she was 135 pounds of limp female meat. Just as she was about to doze, I roused her and we took a shower together. While she was dressing, I said, 'Perhaps your door's not locked.' I went across the hall and tried it. It was open. When I told her, she did not seem very surprised and it occurred to me that she probably knew all along. Perhaps she was even awake when I ventured in the other night.

Thursday, 22 May

I called in sick and took the day off to make sure that everything was ready for my 'interview' with Gertrude. I also called Laura and told her that I was tied up with a special assignment and that I would see her after work tomorrow. We have to be in Garden City tomorrow evening for a wedding rehearsal and a talk with Reverend Fox.

Assailed once again by an unusually fierce appetite, I made myself bacon and eggs, toast and coffee. I had several pieces of toast and heaped them with strawberry jam. I took my second cup of coffee into the living room and lit a cigarette.

With sunlight streaming into the room and the comforting sounds of the city in the distance, I looked over my master list. I kept everything in a file-folder in my attaché case : a carbon of my letter of application, my letters of reference, photographs, autobiography, and even the two pages of my play that I managed to write.

I went over everything carefully. I would check the room at the Saxon Arms to make sure that nothing belonging to Marc was there. I would leave Gertrude's letter on the bureau so that the police could discover it. They would be led there almost certainly by my letter of application. But no, that would only lead them to a post office box. However, my name and photograph would be in their possession. Perhaps it would even appear in the newspapers. I plan to present Gertrude with my 'papers', when I arrive for the interview and to leave them in her apartment by accident. I checked them to see whether or not they contained an address. They did not. I scribbled it on the back of my photograph and then printed it on my curriculum vitae. Was I being too obvious, I wondered. Perhaps some intelligent detective would theorise that I was purposely leaving a trail. But where would his theory lead him if the existence of Claude Elmath couldn't be substantiated?

I tried to picture the whole thing in my mind. I would go up in the elevator, having somehow attracted the attention of the doorman. I would ring the bell. We would go into the living room to talk. I would give her my papers. And then, perhaps while she was looking them over, I would hit her from behind with whatever heavy object was handy. If she were still alive, I would strangle her. But, good lord, what would the motive be? I had stored away the idea of a sexual assault. It was too difficult to think about. Would I, for instance, do it before I killed her or afterwards. Logically, I should bind and gag her so that she could not resist or cry out. But would I tie her hands in front of her or behind her? I tried to think of a reasonable posture in which to have her. My considerations were businesslike but fruitless. Perhaps I should leave cigarette burns on her body to suggest a sadistic madman. But it was all so difficult and I was not at all sure that I could do it. Perhaps I would not be able to perform. Or perhaps she might see through my disguise at such close quarters. Robbery as a motive would be much simpler to arrange. And yet it seemed so unlikely, considering the image of Claude that I was creating in the minds of my pursuers. It was easier for me to imagine Claude Elmath as a respectable bluebeard than as a petty thief. I could hear that nameless detective theorising again : 'A bachelor, afraid of women, suppressed sadistic urges. Suddenly, alone in a room with an attractive widow, he can no longer resist his impulses. He attacks her and kills her. Clearly the murder was spontaneous, not pre-meditated.'

I went back to my list, checking off items with a red pencil. I had to dispose of the printing press now that it had served its purpose. I also had to destroy whatever notes or papers I had accumulated. I made another red mark on my list. And, of course, immediately after the 'interview' I had to dispose of Claude Elmath.

At last, everything seemed ready. I even stuffed a pair of thin leather gloves in my pocket to avoid leaving fingerprints, though it would hardly be a serious matter if the police found a few of my fingerprints in my own mother's apartment. Still, I enjoyed the gesture and felt suddenly quite professional.

All that remained was to find adequate courage to actually confront Gertrude. That was the really difficult part. I thought about it as honestly as I could and gave myself the option of backing out, even at this late date. I offered myself total amnesty, no recriminations. It was a generous offer but I was forced to reject it. As long as Gertrude was alive, I had no future.

At one minute to three exactly, I was rising towards Gertrude in a slow elevator. Bearded and composed I played my part. I had exchanged a few words with the doorman to make sure he would remember me. Now I was trying to get the unwrapped mummy of a Puerto Rican elevator operator to zero in on my existence so that he too might be used as a witness but he kept his eyes fixed on his shoes, as though he were trying to read in their dullness the mysteries of the universe. As we oozed past the fourth floor, I let a half-dollar drop from my hand. He picked it up and offered it to me. 'Keep it,' I said with the coldly generous air of an Englishman in India. He protested, but I motioned for him to open the bloody door. All in all, a sufficient little incident, I thought, to imbed myself in his memory.

As I stood before Gertrude's door, nothing looked really familiar and yet, certainly, I was in the right building standing before the right door. There was her name, just below the bell. I rang and waited. Someone came to the door and looked through the peephole. 'Are you Mr. Elmath?' she said, before opening the latch. 'Yes, indeed I am,' I said, in what seemed an overly loud voice.

'How good of you to be right on time,' she said, leading me down the hall and into the living room. 'Have a seat. Make yourself comfortable.' I chose a straight-backed chair near the window. The light would be behind me. She gave no sign of recognising me, which I suppose should have pleased me, but I found it hard to think about, because I was astounded by the fact that this woman did not in the least remind me of my mother. Her dress was several inches above her knee and she was wearing lipstick. I could not recall ever having seen my mother with lipstick.

I offered her my papers. She accepted them with apologetic shyness, as if to suggest with her fluttering eyelashes that she trusted me to be honest and was only going through a formality, not really checking up on me. Nevertheless, she read my letters of reference carefully and seemed to be studying the signatures. Then she glanced at my curriculum vitae, focusing most of her attention on the photograph I had attached to it. Her lingering over the photograph made me nervous. Suddenly she looked up and said, 'Is this a recent picture?'

'Yes,' I said, 'very recent.'

'Except for the beard you know it doesn't look much like you,' she said. 'I mean it doesn't do you justice.'

I didn't know what to say. Remembering the way Aldo Zappulla raised his eyebrows at the world, I made a kind of European expression that could mean almost anything from astonishment to appreciation. Gertrude seemed amused.

Her manner was friendly and charming. 'And how do you like our country?' she said.

'I've only been here a few weeks,' I said, 'but it's extraordinarily dynamic. Though I must say New York strikes me as a bit hard and a bit grey, not at all like London. Do you know London?'

'I've been there,' she said, apparently fascinated enough by my accent to echo it slightly. In Gertrude's theatrical mind, British English was associated with sophistication. But as far as I could recall, her answer was a lie. That is, she had never been to London, unless it was a secret trip to which she never referred. She was capable of either: the lie or the secrecy. 'It's one of my favourite cities,' she went on, 'in spite of the fog.'

'As you can see from my application,' I said, 'I'm not much for cities. I prefer the country.'

'Lloyd Harbor used to be lovely country,' she said, 'but there's been a lot of building since the war. Incidentally, do you drive?'

'Yes, of course,' I said, 'but I will have to get an American licence.'

There followed a series of quick questions, as though she were trying to catch me off guard: 'Do you have any relatives in America? What kind of a visa do you have? Did you come by plane or boat? Have you done much gardening? Can you sail?'

My galloping horse of a heart balked at that last question and nearly threw me off my seat. I saw us in the *Albatross*, flying before the wind. The perfect murder weapon. And poetically just. I would jib. The boom would crash across, knocking her out and over—and that would be that. Over and out. She would join my father among the crawling monsters of the deep. And I would be free and rich—captain of the *Albatross*.

I recovered my poise sufficiently to say, after an awkward pause, 'Yes, as a matter of fact, I can. Mr. Higgins was very fond of the sea and quite a yachtsman.'

Her face glowed with approval and she looked absolutely girlish and pretty. When she smiled, I could see that she really had teeth. She usually smiled a kind of tight-assed, pinched little smile, a cross between a pucker and a wince, and generally avoided opening her mouth, as though she were afraid that her insides would fall out or that something awful would invade that precious opening. I was suddenly furious that she should treat this bearded English phoney in such a pleasant and congenial manner. What did she imagine she was doing? What sort of a caretaker did she have in mind anyway?

The moment I slipped out of my new role, the moment I allowed myself to think as Marc might think, I was seized with a terrible panic. I imagined that my disguise was falling off or that it was gone entirely. I desperately wanted to look into a mirror. Instead, I touched my beard with a philosophical gesture and tried to talk about one of my plays. There I was back in war-torn Holland again, a wounded R.A.F. tail-gunner. She listened attentively and paid me flirtatious compliments. And then she told me about her brief career on the stage, exaggerating enormously her bit parts and dropping the names of giant stars and directors, some of them dead, as though she saw them every day.

As we talked, I reminded myself that time was slipping away and with it all my opportunities. I commanded myself to act and the command was heard by my obedient adrenal gland. My breath quickened, my eyes darted about the room but kept coming back to Gertrude's smiling face. It was very difficult to talk about one thing and think about another. She kept asking me questions and distracting me from my principal business. I wanted to tell her to shut up for a minute so that I could figure out how to kill her. I was rooted to the chair and had no excuse for getting up. And it seemed rather stupid to sort of throw myself on her in the middle of a sentence. I mean, what if she were too quick for me and slipped away. Besides, I think that along with my British accent I had borrowed a British sense of propriety. Murder was one thing, but it was downright bad manners to interrupt someone while he was speaking.

Still, my conspirator urged me on, taunting me, calling me a weakling and a fool and an English fag. It was Marc, I suppose, struggling to make his puppet do the right thing. 'Do it, man,' he screamed inside of me. 'Do it, do it, do it. Do it now!' And my eyes scanned the room again for a heavy object.

But before I could locate anything, before I could work myself up to the necessary pitch of violence, she was escorting me to the door and pouring instructions and directions in my ear. I was to be at the house in Lloyd Harbor by noon on Sunday so that I could look the place over and decide whether or not I would like the position. We shook hands at the door. Her hand was small and warm in mine, as though I were the parent and she was the child. It's been a long time since I held my mother's hand.

It was only late afternoon by the time I got home, but I took all my clothes off and got into bed. I was so tense that my whole body quivered and I was dizzy. Why had I been unable to carry it off, I kept asking myself. Everything worked beautifully until I actually confronted her. What's wrong with me? Why do I become helpless in her presence?

I dozed for a while, and when I woke up I was in a more reasonable mood. The pain of failure had subsided. The utter self-disgust was gone. I began to see that there were certain flaws in my plan, that there were perfectly logical reasons why

I could not carry out the business. For one thing, I had to be sure she did not scream. In an apartment house, that would be disastrous. I would almost certainly be caught. And then I had not really thought through the actual killing, I mean the physical thing itself. One cannot leave such things to chance. If I was going to hit her I should have carried a weapon. If I was going to strangle her I should have known where to grab her so that she could not cry out. I must be more aggressive, more decisive. I must remember to pick up a book on human physiology. The *Albatross* scheme is out. I can't sustain the role until then.

The seven o'clock news reminded me that there was still a war and still, in fact, a world. It was reassuring in a way. Better a world in chaos than no world at all. I had been so absorbed in my project that I had almost forogtten about outside things. Even Laura had been locked away in another room. I turned the key and let her out. She smiled angelically, superimposed on the face of Spiro Agnew on the TV screen.

As soon as the news was over, I called Laura to remind her that I would pick her up after work tomorrow and that I adored her and thought about her day and night. She said something equally sentimental and we kissed our respective telephones and hung up.

I lit a cigarette and walked back and forth across the room, overwhelmed suddenly by an empty feeling. I didn't know what to do next or even what to think. I was hungry and distracted and depressed. I went to the window to look for my Lady of the Geraniums, but her windows were dark.

Finally, I decided to call my mother. I realised that I was unconsciously waiting for her to call, imagining, for some reason, that I was not allowed to get in touch with her. I dialled her number and waited. She answered after the third ring. We said some routine things and she seemed her normal self. It was clear that she was not going to volunteer any information about her caretaker, so I forced the issue. 'Any more responses to your ad?' I said.

'I interviewed that Englishman today,' she said.

'And how was he?' I said, trying to sound objective.

'Not bad,' she said. 'Not bad at all. In fact, maybe a bit too good for the job.'

'What do you mean?' I said.

'Oh, he's quite intelligent,' she said. 'I don't understand why he's only a caretaker. He could be so much more.'

I felt complimented, but also uneasy. Had I aroused her suspicion by making Claude too talented? It even occurred to me that the whole plan was transparent and that she was just toying with me. Perhaps the invitation to Lloyd Harbor on Sunday was a trap. The moment I made a move to attack her her agents might leap from the walls and disarm me. The whole idea was ridiculous and paranoic. I put it aside. Of course she didn't know. How could she?

Gertrude said there was somebody at her door and we quickly said goodbye. Who was her visitor? I wondered. Perhaps it was Claude, I thought, smiling to myself. Or perhaps it was Uncle Phil.

I could not stop reviewing the absurd events of the day. In my mind I heard every scrap of conversation again. I rose in that coffin-like elevator. I dropped that half-dollar again and again. I studied my mother's name over the bell; I heard her voice through the peephole. It all kept coming back and coming back along with a sense of failure. But with it all, came the rising tide of my sexual desperation. It was a powerful distraction from all my pre-occupations but it was itself a kind of torment. It was like going from the frying pan of the mind to the fire of the body. I itched, I yearned, I burned. I wanted hot flesh. I wanted women.

I did not know who to call. Actually, I knew very few women aside from Laura. I thought of Virginia Workman. I dialled her number nervously, rehearsing my lines. Her apology was incoherent, almost hysterical, and we hung up. I had the feeling that I caught her in the midst of another adventure. Poor girl! She must feel by now that every time she gets laid a bell rings, like a damn Pavlovian dog.

I decided that my best possibility was one of the nurses but they did not get in until quite late. I left my door ajar so that I would be sure to hear the elevator, and settled down to watch a movie on television. Eventually, my Florence Nightingales of the flesh showed up. I waylaid them, so to speak, in the hallway, and invited them in for a drink. They were pleased. They sat at either end of the couch, decorating my dim living room with their crisp, white uniform shapes and pale oval faces. Pink phosphorescent lips opened and closed around their adolescent jokes, long white legs crossed and uncrossed themselves, and starchy bosoms invited the unveiling of the real thing. As with nuns, their costumes seem an armour against reality. I long to penetrate that shiny front and discover the warm smelly flesh beneath it. All women are like that. They create an image of themselves and then wear it like a uniform.

'What do you girls do at the hospital that keeps you so happy?' I asked.

They laughed in stereo and moved like mirror reflections of each other. Pale faces turned together, then apart, then two white arms leapt up to cover the banal giggle that issued from two pink mouths. A reflected ripple from the TV set shimmered across them and their eyes settled once again on me.

'You'd be surprised what goes on in hospitals,' said the blonde one. 'We have—fun.'

We all laughed, and drank again. 'Here's to fun,' I said. I hoped we were moving towards an understanding but I could not be sure. I walked slowly towards them across the carpet, my eyes on the one with whom I was familiar. When I sat between them, I put my arm around her and let my hand fall on her breast. I squeezed it, and smiled at the other girl, the brunette. She had shapely legs, although she was not very tall, and I felt sure that when she stood up her thighs would not touch, a quality which I cherish in the female animal. She smiled back at me, so I reached out my other long arm and said, 'Join the party.' We all laughed again and I felt their hands on me.

I kissed the blonde one, who was rather plump, and then the dark one, and then the blonde one again. I worked my hand under her armpit to feel the roundness of her breast under the sharp material of the uniform. The other girl pretended to be jealous and leaned across my body. She submitted her pale pink mouth for kissing and put her hand over my hand which was feeling the blonde's breast.

'Share the wealth,' she said.

'I'm a born communist,' I said. I stood up. 'Come, my little comrades. We have a meeting of the central committee,' and I led them into the bedroom. I flung myself down on the bed and said, 'I'm a sick man. I need nurses.' Their laughter fell about me like the coins of a slot machine when you hit the jackpot. Their hands were all over me as they undressed me, and they slowly abandoned their nurse act in favour of a more seductive role.

They began to undo buttons and slip out of their clothes. Bodies turned, arms moved, uniforms crackled. Hands behind my head on the pillow, I watched coldly and lustfully. I was the Sultan and they were my handmaidens.

The dark girl had an elegant shape, with a very slim waist, boyish hips and hard small breasts. She was really quite beautiful next to the cow-like blonde. But that one had quantity, a lavish white overflowing softness. I studied her upper thighs and the curve of her buttocks as she dropped her slip and then stepped out of her panties. She sat on the bed and held my hand while we both watched the other finish undressing. She was sitting on a chair to remove her white stockings. Her hands and arms were as delicate as the rest of her. She reached behind her and unhooked her bra. The first sight of her tiny brown nipples contracted my guts. It was not the near perfection of that modest bosom but the sudden nakedness.

In a moment, we were all in bed under a single sheet—my favourite fantasy now a reality. But no sooner did we begin our little ballet of the flesh than I began to feel that depression and disappointment that haunts so many of my sexual encounters. In my confusion my lust was mingled with nausea. I saw us doing the things I dreamed of doing. And it was seeing it as much as doing it that excited me. But then I saw us differently, objectively. Three white little bodies, entwined, worm-like, trying with blind instinct to combine, as if all existence was a collective thing and we were driven by the racial memory of *oneness*. I wanted to cry for us all. Poor me. Poor them. Poor mankind. But I went on. The momentum was too great. It is perhaps what in medieval times they meant by being possessed by the devil. Who knows!

Afterwards, we had coffee and smoked cigarettes. It was very late. I wanted them to leave, but they lingered, softened by passion; motherly and a little concerned about the sad look in my eyes. I assured them that I was the happiest man in the world and stood up to urge them on their way.

Friday, 23 May

I arrived at the office only half an hour late, not nearly as exhausted as I should have been. Hinkle called to ask for some neglected galleys and I promised to dig them out instantly. He was abrupt and irritable. I slammed down the phone and cursed him with muttered eloquence. That flea, that pimple. That presumptuous little non-person. How I hate the tiny, self-important people of the world. I am plagued by them: Gulliver among the Lilliputians. They are too meticulous, too trivial, too unaware of the things that really matter: the heights, the depths, the broad sweep. I could, without conscience, exterminate them all. Surely there must be an insecticide for human pests—*homo pipiens, culex sapiens.* Better genocide than this constant buzzing in the ear. I could imagine a thousand Hinkles queued up for the gas chamber, all of them with the same face, all wearing glasses, all naked and yellow and obediently carrying a little card. Step lively, boys! In you go. No shoving please. Wait your turn There's plenty of room for everyone.

I escaped from the coffee-break commotion by visiting the company library in the basement. I thought if I browsed for a while, something might occur to me. I wandered up and down the aisles of books, clicking lights on and off in the narrow passages, glancing at titles, occasionally taking out a volume to scan the dust jacket or flip through the pages. I was the only one in the room. I felt cool and peaceful and safe from the rattle of business.

The room was dark except for the overhead light in the aisle

I was using. I came to the end of the aisle and switched off the light before switching on the next one. I waited, enjoying the sensation. There were no windows. I could see nothing. I heard the hum of silence. After a while, I wandered away from the switch, feeling my way like a mole in narrow places.

My underground dream was interrupted by an intruder. I heard the heavy door open and close and saw a light go on in the first aisle but I could not see who it was. I lurked in the darkness, afraid to turn on a light, afraid to attract attention. There was a clicking of heels and a clicking of switches. The lights came closer. I went to the end of the last aisle and found that I could not turn the corner as I had done in the others. I was in a blind alley. I waited, feeling my body dampen with perspiration. If it was a girl I was afraid I would kill her. But the footsteps halted. There was a long pause and then they receded again, clicking the aisles into darkness, until the door slammed and I was alone again. It was a strange experience. I don't know how to explain it.

At about eleven-thirty, I was overwhelmed with a great sense of boredom. I kept looking at my watch but it didn't seem to move. Something was either wrong with it or with my own sense of time. Perhaps my inner clock had stopped. Perhaps I would be frozen there for all of eternity behind that pile of papers in that little green, coffin-like cubicle, connected to the outside world only through the umbilical telephone line. I yawned several times, as though I couldn't get enough oxygen out of the air. I seemed to be suffocating.

I tried to think about lunch. I was free for a change. Laura was attending one of those farewells to a pregnant secretary. I thought I might go up to the Saxon Arms for a while, just to keep up appearances, so to speak. And then I thought of Nancy McGuire, the woman in Sammy's bar. Why not? I thought. Something about Claude's relationship with her amused me : the gentleman and the actress, an old theme. I was talking to myself in Claude's voice. I dialled the number and waited, clearing my throat and tucking in my chin. I got the switchboard and asked for Miss McGuire. She took a long time to answer, and when she did it was clearly from her bed. I apologised and waited for her to remember who I was—and possibly who she was. I suggested lunch and from inside the barrel of nicotine, alcohol, and general failure, she accepted. I was delighted and flattered, not because the lady was fair, but simply because she accepted Claude's existence.

As I went out, I told Linda I'd be back around two. 'Who's the guy who was just in there?' she said. 'I didn't see him come in. A guy with an English accent. I didn't see him go out either.'

I must have blushed visibly at my blunder, but I faced up to her. 'There hasn't been anybody here all morning,' I said. 'Just me. You must be hearing things.'

She frowned and chewed her gum very rapidly but said nothing. For once her inability to think was an asset.

In the non-theological sense of the homosexual phrase, lunch with Nancy McGuire was *divine*. I had expected one of those purgatorial plunges into the darker parts of human experience and exposure to human frailty and disease that both depresses and exalts. Instead, I discovered that this wilted Irish rose still had a lot of the juice and joy of life in her and was, in many ways, an attractive human being.

We went to a little Italian restaurant not far from the Saxon Arms, and once inside, seated at a simple table with its red-checkered tablecloth, we might have been anywhere in America or Europe. Nancy did not over-dress, as I was afraid she might; nor did she smell of the wrestling match of fragrances and odours that so often typify the bar-room lush. She was actually clean and her eyes were clear. I marvelled at the efficiency of her liver and kidneys and gave high marks also to her circulatory system. Her antique hairstyle and loose white dress brought to mind such cinema dames as Jean Harlow and Alice Faye.

Naturally, I was a bit self-conscious. It was, in a sense, my first date. I was a fifty-five year-old adolescent, with hair instead of acne on my face. I selected a table along a wall on which there was a large mirror that had painted on it churches and gondolas and other things Italian. In an unpainted space, I could see myself in the mirror, as though I were a drowned man looking up from a polluted canal. I kept glancing towards Venice all during our lunch, eager to see how I looked in the eyes of other people —from the outside.

We had wine with our lunch and my confidence grew. My accent became slightly more British and less Canadian. Nancy told me about her childhood in Boston, about how she was one of seven children and how her father drank himself to death during the depression. At fifteen, she ran away from home, took a job as a waitress, having lied about her age and began her adventures. She was almost instantly raped by the Portuguese cook. She lived with a juggler, she married a drummer, she mothered twins, one of whom died, she did chorus-line bits, a little singing and dancing in musicals, and then, finally, straight stripping. Her husband disappeared. She married again, without the benefit of a divorce. She had another child, whom she deposited with her sister in Springfield, and continued her long flight to climb from the gutter to the kerbstone of the theatrical world.

Nancy's chronicle was punctuated with girlish gustatory sounds that could only come from someone who grew up hungry and was trying to fill her empty child's belly retroactively.

'I can see you've had a difficult life,' I said. 'My dear, the world is full of injustice.'

She tried to look embarrassed, dabbing at gravy and lipstick with the corner of her napkin. 'Have I been talking too much about myself?' she said. 'I mean, I've practically told you the history of my life and we hardly know each other. And I bet your life hasn't been too easy either, has it?'

I think she meant it as a compliment, as if a hard life were a badge of honour of some kind. 'Oh, it hasn't been too bad,' I said. 'Some good times; some bad times.'

She stared at me. 'How long have you had your beard?' she said.

I was startled and consulted the face in the Venetian canal to see if it was also startled. It looked back at me with the composure of a Greek philosopher, a stoic thoroughly prepared for disaster or death. 'Since after the war,' I said. 'Why do you ask?'

118

'Oh, I don't know,' she said, tilting her head. 'I was just wondering how you would look without it.'

'Why? Don't you like it?' I said.

'Oh, no, don't get me wrong,' she said. 'I like it. I love it. It's so—you know—distinguished. You look like that guy who sells Schweppes—what's his name?'

'Commander Whitehead,' I said. 'The resemblance is purely coincidental. I have, as a matter of fact, considered shaving it off from time to time but now that beards have come back in style, I think I will keep it.'

'I'm glad,' she said, smiling and glancing at the menu. We ordered some zabiglioni and espresso. She went back to her rambling adventures, all her sharp edges softened by a full belly.

I smoked my pipe and she smoked cigarettes, leaving little red smudges on the filter tips. I reminded myself that she would make a marvellous witness when the police came around to make their inquiries. I glanced at my watch and she asked me if I was late for work or something. 'At the moment I am unemployed,' I said, and then described my prospects on Long Island.

'Gee, I hope it works out for you,' she said, genuine warmth in her Irish eyes. Her hand crept across the table to where mine was. Out of the corner of my eye, her fingertips dripped with blood. It was a heavy hand with stubby fingers, the hand of a scrubwoman or a farmer's wife. I did not retreat from the gesture. 'You deserve a break. You're such a nice guy. Most guys are creeps with only one thing in mind. But you're different.'

The restaurant had emptied out except for us. 'I guess it's time to go,' I said.

She looked suddenly distracted, afraid perhaps that I was about to abandon her. 'Look,' she said, 'why don't we go up to my place for a drink?'

Back in her room at the Saxon Arms, a room much like my own, she poured us a drink and we sat on the bed. Though perhaps not the most articulate person in the world, Nancy soon made herself clear. 'Look,' she said, 'we're not getting any younger, so there's no sense in beating around the bush. You showed me a good time today and I'm willing to show you a good time. What do you say?'

Though I had already guessed what was coming, I did not imagine that it would come so quickly and so bluntly. I was suddenly as nervous as a real virgin. I felt awkward. Cautiously I drew her to me and kissed her. When I backed away, I half expected my beard to have been shifted from my face to hers. But it was still intact and she was smiling warmly as though she had been kissed by a real man.

We undressed and got into bed. Everything would be fine, I thought, as long as she did not try to run her fingers through my hair. My posture was formal and my movements a little clumsy but I could blame all that on being British. However, Nancy took it all as gentility, after her long experience with 'drunken slobs' as she called them, and actually enjoyed our little fox trot of a fuck, heaving herself around like a lazy surf to help along my slow rhythms. We took our pleasure in a decorous middle-aged way and then lay back to smoke and think about it. I suspect that Nancy's thoughts were interlaced with antipasto and lasagna. But it was all right. It was all very nice and I enjoyed it more than I might have imagined.

After changing roles, I went back to the office, feeling such a mixture of ages: I was the boy of sixteen after his first great sexual encounter; I was the mature, indifferent bachelor, on whose list of conquests this trivial incident was barely worth inclusion; I was the middle-aged man who was beginning to be afraid that he would never make love again.

It was difficult to work but I did routine things for an hour or so, while Linda avoided me and I avoided Hinkle. I think that Linda is beginning to suspect that there is something odd about me. However, I have faith in her essential thickness of mind. I do not believe the thought exists that can penetrate deeply enough to become a real idea. As for Hinkle, I couldn't care less. In the immortal words of Nancy McGuire, 'Piss on him!'

After work, I took a subway uptown. It was very crowded and I was bundled together with two sweating women. One of them tried to ram her elbow into the pit of my stomach to protect her personal space, as though in that plunging subterranean phallus there really was such a thing as personal space. Madness. The woman was mad. The three million sperm I spit into the slimy darkness of a woman have more personal space then those of us who ride the subway.

I picked up Laura and we went on to the garage where I keep my car. She was all smiles and affection, though I detected a certain tension in her. She sat very close to me and held my arm as though she was afraid I was going to get away before the wedding. After all, I was at least as vital an ingredient in that ceremony as her gown or the flowers or the minister himself.

There was a long delay on the Long Island Expressway. Bumper-to-bumper we crept past that vast city of the dead in Queens, that endless graveyard, so crowded and depressing. We lingered in carbon-monoxide fumes, the sun a hazy orange globe in the poisoned air.

After a while, the traffic moved more quickly and before long we were in Garden City. We stopped at a bakery to pick up something for dessert. We were in the shop for less than a minute when I almost had an orgasm. The air was charged with warmth and sweetness, the fragrance of freshly baked bread, yeast, butter and assorted spices. We were immersed in whipped cream and powdered sugar. Immense strawberries leapt at us out of their tarts and shortcakes and the heaped up cookies were a child's dream of paradise. Behind the counter, waiting for us to choose, was a healthy, homely young frau, all plump and good enough to eat, with apples for cheeks, cantelopes for breasts, white and starched and inviting us with her luscious smile to plunge in, as though into a sea of totally satisfying oral delight.

Laura chose the blueberry cheese cake and I nodded my approval, too afraid to speak or move, trembling on the brink of a spasm. I don't understand what's wrong with me these days. Everything excites me sexually. The world is full of aphrodisiacs. I sometimes, for instance, visit the supermarket just to look at all that food and all those women. I put a few things in a basket and wheel it around, shopping not for provisions but for thighs and breasts and damp red lips and flashes of naked skin. I linger among the vegetables; I study the mounds of fruit.

The wedding party assembled at the Haleys' for dinner. It was all painfully boring. Afterwards, we went to the church to see Reverend Fox. He took me and Laura into his office and we had an earnest little chat about values and God and life. He's a sober sort, old Reverend Fox, a man about sixty, who gave me the impression that he didn't really believe in marriage. Marriage had a way of throwing men and women together and when men and women are thrown together they have a depressing tendency to fuck. It was this part of the whole situation that seemed to be foremost in his dirty mind, though he could not, in our brief interview, find the words with which to name it. He was trying to tell us that God created sex purely as a means of procreation and it ought not to become an indulgence for its own sake. It was quite clear that Reverend Fox was against pleasure, especially sexual pleasure. I wondered how Mrs. Fox felt about all this.

Since our ceremony is going to be extremely simple, the rehearsal did not take long. Still, it gave me an odd feeling to approach the altar, to stand beside that pretty young woman, to hear spoken over us words encrusted with time and tradition and, presumably, wisdom. The church was musty and the lights were dim. If there really were a God, I wondered, would things be simpler or more difficult?

In my expanding catalogue of aphrodisiacs, I must include churches. I would like some day to make love in a church, preferably in a darkened choir loft or behind the organ while a service was going on below and preferably to the minister's teenage daughter, a girl with rock-like breasts and uncontrollable passions.

The wedding party dispersed and I went off into the night, a lonely figure in a small foreign car, to face my difficult problem. I was only partly cheered when, back in my apartment, I discovered that my Lady of the Geraniums was still awake and that her blinds had not yet been drawn.

Saturday, 24 May

I woke to summer sweetness, having spent the night in oblivion. My dreamless sleep was a sample of death and I might have concluded, were it a winter morning, that perhaps it was not so bad after all. But it was not a winter morning and my senses were assailed by life. Sun streaked through the blinds and blazed in the mirror. I could feel the warm air through the open window and sense the general juice of spring—spring big with the child of summer.

Laura called while I was still in bed. Her voice was crisp and clean and I felt the surge of the day in her. 'Let's go to the beach,' she chirped, and I answered her song with sleepy kisses.

Like most sensible neurotics I am afraid of the sea, but fascinated by it. 'Going to the beach', however, means more than staring into the hypnotic surf. It means sun and heat and human flesh. And all that nakedness makes me nervous. I can't read or doze or listen to the radio. All I can do is stare longingly at female bodies. While Laura submits passively to the sun's embrace, I twitch and squirm and strain my eyes. I make excuses to walk down the beach or through the dunes. I sit ten feet away from lonely women and try psychically to explain to them that I too am lonely.

This time I was assaulted by waves of passion and sadness. At times, I felt a oneness with the little race of men. There we all were, a fleshy, pathetic, self-conscious species, stretched out, trance-like, on the sand, as though we were trying to remember our origins in the sea. Sometimes I imagine I can look down on us all, as though from a great height, from some invisible blue ledge in the endless sky. I see us as a cluster of maggots, squirming and uneasy, as though, in the beginning, God lifted a great rock and discovered us there. What a peculiar organism man is, striving to be separate and alone, but yearning to collect, to gather, to merge, to return to the simple harmony of his earlier times, before the central nervous system, before intelligence, before the fall.

When the Haleys decided to go *en famille* to the local cinema this evening, I made up a desperate story about an editorial emergency I had to cope with immediately and went home. Excited and exhausted by my first exposure this year to public nudity and flushed from several hours in the sun, I arranged myself on the couch with a tall drink and a cigarette.

When the doorbell rang, it was almost ten o'clock. I half expected it to be my giddy nurses ready for a return engagement. But it was someone else—a young woman in a long dress, open at the neck and tattered at the hem. She was carrying a dead flower and might have walked out of a Pre-Raphaelite painting into the awfulness of the present. Her hair was loose and framed her delicate face. And there was a distracted air about her. She was a Burne-Jones lady all right but one who had been running wild and barefooted through the streets of Greenwich Village. It took me half a minute to realise that it was my cousin Emily.

I took her by the hand and led her to the couch. She was limp and unsteady. Her eyelids drooped and she smiled as though she was drunk or high on drugs. 'What's happened to you?' I said.

She tilted her head and looked at me. 'Happened?' she said, her voice and eyebrows rising. 'Happened? Nothing ever happens to me. Nothing ever happens to anybody.' She waved her dead flowers in my direction. It was an enormous lily, shrivelled and brown at the edges.

'Where did you get that?' I said.

She held the flower too close to her face and stared into it. 'Lilies that fester smell far worse than weeds,' she recited over dramatically. 'Funeral wedding,' she said and laughed. 'Funeral wedding. Do you take this woman and all that.'

'What have you been drinking?' I said.

She stood up and wandered around the room, floating, then dancing, her airy gown like a négligé following her in slow motion. 'Absinthe,' she said. 'Absinthe makes the heart grow fonder.' She laughed again and swatted imaginary flies with her dead lily.

'Where have you been?' I said, impatient with this little drama of hers. 'What have you been doing? Why are you running around barefooted?' I moved towards her, but she waltzed away, pausing beside the lamp and flirting with it like a moth.

'Come your ways. Come your ways,' she laughed. The light from the lamp caught her face at an odd angle and her eyes blazed out of shadows. It occurred to me that she might be genuinely insane.

Though I was angry at her performance and resented her coming to my apartment unexpectedly, I forced myself to speak gently to her. 'Now take it easy,' I said. 'There's nothing to be afraid of. Sit down and have a drink and tell me why you came here.'

She stood still in the middle of the room, her wild eyes darting here and there. 'Why? Why? Because "He hath, my lord, of late made many tenders of his affections to me." '

'What are you talking about?' I said.

And she went on. ' "Like a green girl unsifted in such perilous circumstances." '

I moved towards her, anger uncoiling in me like a snake. I knew I should be kind. I knew she was in trouble and that I should soothe her but my impulse was to catch her and beat her and kick her. Maybe even strangle her and cut her into little pieces. What is it about my poor cousin that invites laceration? Surely she was doing all this to provoke me. There is nothing more annoying than this kind of imposition. This forcing of oneself on another person. This demand to be recognised. Why can't she cuddle her misery in private?

She eluded me as I reached for her, dodging away behind the leather chair. 'Emily,' I said. 'Come and sit down. Come and talk to me.' I stalked her, moving cautiously, the way one is taught to move in the woods. Then I lunged at her, tipping over the chair, but missing her. The chair went down like an old elephant, slowly and with an overstuffed thud. I cursed and sprang up again. 'Emily,' I said. 'Emily, don't act like this. It's all an act, isn't it?'

She had gotten behind the couch and used it as a barrier. Safe for the moment she mocked me. 'Emily. Emily. Dear Cousin Emily.' And then she broke into a little Elizabethan song:

'Young men will do't, if they come to't;
By cock, they are to blame.
Quoth she, before you tumbled me
You promised me to wed.'

She fiddled with her buttons as she sang and undid them unconsciously until the front of her dress was opened almost to her waist.

'Have you come back for more?' I said. 'Is that it? Or have you come to tell me your little secret?' I followed her around the couch, first one way then the other. 'Well, if it's more you want, you'll have to stand still. You can't expect me to make love to you on the run.' There was a sinister tone creeping into my voice. My eyes narrowed. I swallowed curses.

' "Rich gifts wax poor when givers prove unkind," ' she said, and tore open her dress to reveal her naked breasts. A dark storm swept across her face. 'Come on,' she said. 'Come on and get me. Take me. Do what you want to me. Ruin me. Kill me. Fuck me. Anything. Anything.' She was screaming and laughing and crying all at once.

I knew now she wouldn't run away. I came up to her, put my arm around her and led her to the couch. 'Would you like some coffee?' I said.

'No,' she said. 'I want *you*. Don't you understand?'

I sat down beside her. Her face was damp now, but still quivered with broken smiles and suppressed hysterical laughter. 'I've loved you since I was a little girl. You didn't know that, did you? I dreamed about marrying you. I used to play house. You were the daddy, the teddy bear, and I was the mommy and we had children. We had ten children. They were rag dolls and toy animals. And then it almost came true. Almost!'

126

She lunged at me and wrapped her arms fiercely about my neck. 'Kiss me!' She screamed. 'Kiss me!' Her pathetic face banged against mine. She was like a desperate kitten, searching for her mother's breast. I pushed her away, but she resisted, her arms locked around me.

'Stop it, Emily,' I said, reaching back to pull away her arms. 'You're making a damned fool of yourself.'

Her eyes were closed and she kept repeating, 'Kiss me. Kiss me. Love me.'

I didn't know I was going to hit her but suddenly my fist was clenched and it shot out in a short jab that caught her in the softness of her belly. She fell away from me with a moan. 'I'm sorry,' I said. 'I'm sorry.'

She had difficulty getting her breath. Clutching herself she looked at me as though I had betrayed her. Her mouth revealed her bitterness and disgust. 'You monster,' she gasped. 'You goddamned cruel son-of-a-bitch. Why don't you go all the way? Why don't you kill me? Come on, lover, kill me. This is kill-your-cousin week. Don't be afraid. Take your knife and stick it here.' She slapped at her naked chest.

'Shut up,' I said. 'That's enough. You're imagining things. You're hysterical.'

'Sure I am,' she said, getting up again. 'I'm the hysterical type. Didn't you know. Struck dumb by an unhappy childhood.'

I went after her and grabbed her by the arms. 'Struck dumb by what?' I said threateningly. 'By what?'

She went pale and sobered slightly. 'By nothing. Besides, what's the difference? The past is dead.'

I shook her hard. 'This time you'll tell me,' I said. She could see that I meant it. 'What was it? Come on, tell me.'

She shook her head and tried to pull away. I slapped her and she went into her crazy act again, singing her old songs : 'By Gis and by Saint Charity/Alack, and fie for shame!' And then my open hand descended again, cracked against her jaw and drew blood from her mouth. She gagged and coughed but tried to go on singing. I hit her again, this time with my fist. She fell to the rug, dazed but still humming. I picked her up and dragged her roughly to the couch. She submitted. I stretched her out and, breathing heavily, I leaned close to her and said, 'Now, Cousin Emily, tell me.' My hand crept towards her white throat.

She looked weary and indifferent all of a sudden and her eyes rolled up under her lids. I thought she was fainting. But then she started to talk, as if in a dream or a trance. 'Mommy took me on a train. Mommy talked. She pulled at me. Hurry. Hurry. Watch your white shoes. Don't drag your feet. Grandma. Grandma's waiting at the station. Why was Daddy mad? I said. He threw money at her. Take it, he said. Take it all. And it fell around us like dead birds. She cried. We were on the train and a black man came and gave us orange juice and sandwiches. His breath was peppermint and he had white teeth. A whistle blew. A bell clanged at the crossing. The train jerked. Mommy read a book and looked out the window. It was a mirror. There were two mommies. She had a handkerchief in her hand. And I woke up and we were there. It was dark and somebody put me in a car. The trees were monsters. There were chickens behind a fence. Grandma smelled of old flowers and the piano had a roll of paper in it. They talked in the kitchen and drank tea. Go to bed, dear, she kept saying, and I watched the roll go round and round with little holes in it and the keys played by a ghost—plink, plunk, plink, plink. And the cat he hated me with green eyes. And they said, be quiet. And I was alone with flowers growing out of the wall and rain on the roof in the small room. In the morning, Mommy drank coffee on the porch, and an old man with no teeth talked to us through the screen. Then Grandma gave us a basket full of flowers and tomatoes and we went to the train. Mommy smoked cigarettes and the smoke was blue in the sunshine. I blew it away. Click, clack, click, clack, went the train and it got dark. I fell asleep. It's all right. It's all right, said Mommy. We're home now. And the elevator went up. I thought we were still in the train. She took my hand. We came to the door and she looked for her key. I was hungry. I held my teddy bear and waited. She turned the key and we went into the dark. At first there was no noise but there was a light in the hallway from the bedroom. Mommy turned on the light and somebody called, Who's there? There was another voice. Mommy ran, screaming. In the bedroom there were three voices. Mommy dropped her purse. I held my teddy bear against my face and followed her. Daddy was naked and there was a lady in the bed. They were all screaming. Daddy hit Mommy. Mommy fell down. She got up and ran. She knocked a chair over. I hid in the closet and I could smell Daddy's coat and the umbrellas. When I came out, Mommy was gone and Daddy took me in his arms and said, Don't worry, baby. Don't worry. Forget all this. Never say anything. It will be all right. Everything will be all right.

'I looked for the lady but she wasn't there. Daddy put me to bed. He kissed me and put out the light. You must promise never to say anything, he said again, his face close to mine and breathing heavy and fast like our old dead dog. It was very dark and I was afraid. I was afraid all night and it was a long long time until morning came. And in the morning Mommy was still gone. And she never came back.'

Emily opened her eyes.

'What else?' I said.

'Nothing,' she said. 'I don't remember.' She sat up.

'The woman in the bed,' I said. 'Who was the woman in the bed?'

'I don't know,' she said.

'What did she look like?' I said breathlessly.

'I don't know,' she repeated. 'I can't remember.'

'Think hard,' I said. 'Think. Try to remember. Was it my mother? Was it your Aunt Gertrude?'

She looked away, frowning, desperately trying to dredge up that strange woman, that intruder. 'I don't know. I don't know,' she said. 'It could have been. I was too young. I was too frightened. She didn't say anything. She looked as though she had just been stabbed.'

I took Emily by the arms and shook her hard. Her head thumped against the back of the couch. 'Think,' I shouted. 'Think, you little idiot. It was my mother, wasn't it? Say it! Admit it! Don't try to spare me. Go on. Say it. Say it.' I was hitting her again.

Emily was crying and struggling. Her hands tried to bend back my fingers, which were at her throat. 'All right, all right,' she moaned. 'It was your mother. It was whoever you want it to be.'

I let her go and she collapsed into her own lap, shuddering and sobbing. 'I'm sorry,' I said, standing up and collecting myself. 'I'm sorry, Emily. I didn't mean to hurt you.' I walked away from her and lit a cigarette with violently trembling hands. 'But it's important. You have no idea how important it is.'

Her sobbing subsided as she slumped into the cushions of the couch. 'Emily!' I called, but she didn't answer or move. I was sure that I had killed her. I rushed to her and shook her, shouting her name hysterically in her face. Then I was insanely angry again. I wanted to kill her for being dead. I hit her and saw the blood ooze from her lower lip. Then I heard her moan and I realised that she was alive. I picked her up and carried her into the bedroom. I put her between the white sheets and tucked her in like a child. With a damp cloth I washed her bruised face. She did not wake up. I left her alone and lay down on the couch to collect myself.

I fell asleep and when I woke up again there was a hint of daylight around the edge of the closed blinds. I got up, feeling enormously heavy, and staggered to the bedroom door. Emily was gone. The only traces of her were several small bloodstains on the pillow. I would have to get rid of those, I thought and began to assemble myself for the important events that were coming.

Sunday, 25 May

Armed with Emily's account of my mother's infidelity—practically incestuous—I assumed my murderer's role and went forth, with all the forces of good on my side, to remove that vile woman from the face of the world.

I rented a Volkswagen and drove out to Lloyd Harbor. It was a longish ride, which gave me time to think. Though I started out bravely, so many terrible possibilities occurred to me en route that I was about to abandon the whole project and resign myself to my disinheritance, my emotional bondage, and a life of quiet desperation, feeling girls in the office and drinking myself to sleep at night. I was haunted by the idea that somewhere along the line I had made a serious mistake, left a disastrous clue, though I could not think what it might be. My head seemed to be contracting. My eyes felt heavy and sticky. I heard a ringing in my ears.

Perhaps Gertrude already knows, I thought, and an icy panic gripped my bowels. Perhaps she, too, is keeping a diary. Perhaps she has been on to me all along. She is perfectly capable of having me watched by private detectives. Is it possible that all these years I have been followed by one of her agents, that my phone has been tapped, that she has been fully aware of all my little adventures? On the other hand, she would hardly have invited me out to such a secluded place if she really thought she were in any danger.

By the time I was driving up West Neck Road into Lloyd Harbor, I had recovered sufficient confidence to believe, once again, that I could do what I had come to do. It would be much simpler here in the country, without the danger of interference.

As I walked up the cobbled path to the Tudor style house, a woman greeted me. It was that other Gertrude, the smiling, middle-aged, former actress. She was wearing over-sized sunglasses and a large, limp straw hat. Since I knew this woman was not my mother, I was not at first disturbed by her pink abbreviated overalls. It was Marc who first recognised her, not Claude, and from somewhere inside the dashing Englishman Marc growled, 'You slut, you whore, you double-dealing bitch. Seduce the caretaker, will you! Pretending all these years to be my good old mother, my mean, neat, nervous mother, a woman of absolute virtue devoted to charitable causes.' But Claude took her hand when she extended it and responded to her smile with a smile. Marc receded.

Gertrude showed me through the house and around the grounds. They were, of course, thoroughly familiar to me. She was particularly eager that I should see the caretaker's cottage. It seemed clear to me that it was all settled in her mind and that she was determined to have me as 'her man' so to speak.

Back in the main house, I stood in the kitchen with her while she made us some tall drinks. She crushed ice, ran the blender, sliced lemons, and so on, with the efficiency and swiftness that one could only expect from a woman who loved her kitchen. 'Don't you believe it,' yelled Marc. 'It's all part of a big, bloody seduction scene.' In that instant, some forces in me came together and everything seemed clear and bright and straightforward. There was the knife on the counter, wet with lemon juice. There was Gertrude in front of the refrigerator, wondering for a second where the maraschino cherries were. The pink straps criss-crossed against the white blouse, making a sort of target. A hundred thousand years passed in that instant. Rome rose and fell. Helen was carried away. Huns and Vandals and Mongols thundered across the world. And then the knife was in my hand. Desperate images were clicked out along the wires of my brain, like calls for help from a colonial outpost. Hundreds of little muscles quivered and stumbled, trying to co-ordinate themselves into the right response to the right signal. And then, as my arm was about to raise itself, about to carry out a dimly-heard command, she turned and faced me, holding in her hand the jar of very red cherries. Her smile faded into a frown. Her eyes blinked several times. 'Is anything wrong?' she said. I saw the hollow at the base of her throat and her collarbones spreading into her white blouse. I handed her the knife with butler-like calm and said, 'Perhaps you can use this to get them out. You know, stab them with the point.' She blushed and accepted the knife without further comment.

It is quite possible that she thought nothing of the whole incident, since it was largely an incident in my own mind. In any case, we had lobster salad for lunch on the patio and talked about the caretaker's duties and about ourselves and the terrible state of the modern world. It was, in spite of the odd circumstances, a very pleasant afternoon. And, because I was unable to produce an adequate excuse, I agreed to begin my employment next Sunday, the first of June.

I drove to a bar on Route 25A in Huntington, a place I used to go to occasionally years ago. I was halfway through my second drink before I fully realised what had happened. I had had the opportunity but I had failed to do the deed. I was discovering areas of weakness in me that I did not believe existed. But I was also beginning to realise that my reactions as Claude were not the same as my reactions as Marc. I not only acted differently but I had different feelings. Claude, for instance, is much more benign and generous. And Claude is somewhat flattered by Gertrude's seductive manner. Marc, of course, is outraged by the whole thing and broods murderously. Marc thinks Claude is a fool and Claude thinks Marc is a lecherous swine.

By the time I had finished my third drink, I felt that I had come to the heart of the matter and I relaxed, as though in a warm bath of complete understanding. I could not seriously accept the idea that I was dividing myself in two. Behind all the make-up and acting, and beyond a certain emotional confusion, I knew I was solidly myself. I could, in fact, feel myself inside myself, as though my body were only a cloak or a suit of clothes. It was the *essential self*, the spark, the core, the inner voice that says *I am*. Both Claude and Marc are roles that I act out—Claude more so than Marc, of course. But even Marc requires a good deal of acting and pretence. He is created on the stage of life: in the office, in bed, at the altar with Laura. I am not a madman with multiple personalities; I am an actor trying to play two roles simultaneously. And I am a good actor, an honest actor, one who, in a sense, lives his part. How else can it be done?

Halfway through my next drink, the flaw in my plan became crystal clear and I felt an uncontrollable smile creep across my face. My revelation was simple: there was no need for all that conversation, all that verbal intercourse. The more we talked the more elaborate Claude's role became. It was distracting. It undermined my original plan. Originally, Claude was meant to be convincing to the outside world, not to Gertrude. Once in the house, like a weasel in a chicken coop, he should be all bloody murder. One can not go through gallant postures and still be a vulgar killer. How foolish to apologise for the plunging knife! No, no, I had carried it all too far, this Claude Elmath business. Some kind of an unconscious delaying tactic, a trick of the mind.

I finished my drink—my fourth or fifth—and slid cautiously from the stool. I found myself remarkably sober and calm. I went out into the dying afternoon. The traffic rushed by in four lanes on Route 25A, swollen bullets of steel moving in slow-motion towards uncertain targets in both the east and west. On the portal of my mind I hung my new motto: 'Consider it not so deeply lest it make you mad.' And I climbed into my rented car and drove back to my mother's house.

My new plan was an arrow in the heavy bow of my will. I would enter the house unseen, having armed myself with a weapon from the tool shed, and attack her from behind.

I parked my car on a dirt road a hundred yards from the house and cut through the woods along a path that emerged between the cottage and the shed. It was a path I used often as a child, imagining, in my loneliness, scouting missions and Indian wars. What magnificent savages had ambushed me along that trail! And oh, how I murdered them into their happy hunting ground in the sky, firing my cap-gun from the hip and cutting their throats with my rubber knife.

The path had grown narrow and was almost reclaimed by nature. I guarded my face from branches and stepped carefully past the brambles. A breeze stirred in the early summer leaves over my head and I could feel the dampness of the woods at sunset. Orange fire tinted the sky against deepening blue. For a moment I was distracted by the silence and the fragrance of the place. I wanted to stop where I was and sit down and stay there forever. I had little boys' thoughts of tree-houses and survival in the wilderness. I could build a fire with a piece of flint. I could gather nuts and berries and make a shelter out of logs. Oh, how marvellous it would be. And of course, it would be forever, because nothing ever really changes and nobody ever really dies.

There was a light on in the kitchen of the house and Gertrude's car was parked in the driveway. I made my way to the shed, keeping an eye on the lighted windows and the back porch. Since the door of the shed faced the house, there was a certain risk of exposure involved. I went quickly to the door, but found it padlocked shut. I should have known. I should have remembered. The key to the ancient brass lock was on a nail inside the pantry door. I glanced again towards the kitchen and saw a figure move quickly past the window. I retreated into the shadows. There was a window in the rear wall of the shed and I had dim memories of forcing it open—for what childish-criminal purpose I could not recall. Worn with age and weather, the windows were loose in their frame. I pried them apart with a stick until the latch separated and I could raise the lower sash.

I climbed into the musty place, blinded by the darkness, and knocked over a watering can. I crouched and held my breath and listened. I could feel, even in the darkness, that the place was crowded with accumulated junk, things that one imagines one will one day need again, things outgrown or replaced but too good to throw away, things intended for yard sales or the Salvation Army.

I waited for a while in my boyish-animal position. When nothing happened, when no bells rang or sirens blew, when no vans of police with sub-machine guns arrived, when no bloodhounds bellowed at the door, I stood up and struck a match. In that flicker of light, I was assailed by familiar and rusty things. Time and dust could not disguise them. I knew my rocking-horse when I saw it, by God! The horse I called Big Red. He was smaller, of course, than when I named him but he still had that wild look on his face, his eyes wide, his mouth open—half terror, half joy. I could feel again the thrill in my groin as I rocked him to the brink of disaster.

The match burned my finger and I let it fall. It was dark again. I needed a candle or a lamp. I needed a weapon—an axe, a piece of pipe, a pair of shears, a pitchfork, anything sharp enough or heavy enough. I lit another match and made my way to the workbench where the tools were. There I found a stub of a candle and lit it. The past emerged again. Ambitious spiders tried to capture the bedsprings on which I used to lie as a child. I recognised the green headboard. O, Clara! I moved to the right and saw a collage of appliances: a toaster, a radio, a cumbersome orange-squeezer, some lamps. Beyond them there were boxes of books. I bent down to see the titles. They were among the first real books I had ever read: old Tom Swifts and Hardy Boys and Tarzans, purchased at rummage sales or handed down from Uncle Phil. I remembered how I used to get up at dawn and read furiously until it was time to go to school.

On the workbench, I spotted a small bundle of trading cards. They were pictures of baseball players, bound together with a piece of string. I broke the string and looked through the cards, my head swimming with nostalgia and nausea. How dumb childhood is, I thought. How pointless and dumb! Do we all collect things like that at the age of ten? What dreams of power, of utopia, of eternal bliss, if only we can get all the cards, all the players. I looked at the faces of the smiling athletes of a quarter of a century ago. I wondered how many of them were still alive. Their names were painfully familiar: Dixie Walker, Ernie Lombardi, Red Schoendienst, Boudreau, Crosetti, Martin, Holmes, Rosen, Kurowski. Good Lord! Oh, Christ! The voice of Red Barber on the radio. Milk and doughnuts after school.

And those playing cards stacked by teams on the chenille spread. How important the Brooklyn Dodgers were. Ghosts of real headlines still stalk me at night, trapped in the dark recesses of my memory cells: Dodgers Win, 4–2, after losing to Pirates as Rally Fails, 4–3.

I stuffed the cards in my pocket and moved away from the dusty books. I scolded myself for being sentimental. One should never think about the past. One should, especially, never think about childhood. Innocence is pathetic. We can't look back without seeing childish dreams crucified on the cross of harsh reality. Childhood is always sad.

I reminded myself that I needed a weapon and searched in the corner where we used to keep the gardening tools. I found a hoe and a rake and a few spades. Beside them was a length of heavy chain. I picked it up. Certainly, that would do. It felt lethal in my hand. Yes, that would do very nicely, I thought, but perhaps an axe would be better, easier to wield and more deadly. I put the chain down and hunted for an axe. I found a large one behind a roll of chicken wire. I picked it up and hefted it. Was it also left over from my childhood, I wondered. And then I tried to imagine how I might use such a clumsy instrument on Gertrude. I couldn't very well hack at her as though she were a tree, chipping pieces out of her thigh or side until she came toppling down. No, I would have to hit her on the head. And suddenly I saw myself creeping up behind her and tapping her on the top of the head with the blunt side of the axe. The logical thing to do then would be to cut off her head, of course. And I could see myself dragging her on to the porch, so that I could hang her head over the first step.

I put out the candle and stepped out of the window of the shed. There was no longer any light in the sky and the moon had not yet come up. I could not tell how long I had been inside. Too long, I was afraid and rushed towards the house. All the lights were out. I stopped short and stared blankly towards the kitchen window. I could feel myself frowning, as though I didn't quite understand. Then I was startled by the sound of an automobile starting up. The motor raced and headlights and taillights popped on. She's still here, I screamed triumphantly to myself and rushed towards her car with the axe raised high. But I was too late. I was within twenty or thirty feet of her when the car shot away, its wheels spinning the loose gravel. I cursed and hurled the axe into the night. It landed harmlessly in the road.

I picked it up and carried it back to the toolshed, muttering to myself about my stupid hesitations and delays. Perhaps it was the alcohol that did it—I mean distorted my sense of time.

I had a key to the main house and went inside to find myself a drink. Then, I went to my mother's room. I don't know what I expected to find there. Certainly, if there ever was any evidence that she had killed my father, she would have destroyed it ages ago. I pushed open the door and went in. My steps were soundless on the thick rug. The darkness smelled of cologne and soap. I snapped on the light and looked around. It's a large room with French doors that go out to a terrace. It is full of pastels and lace. The bed is a four-poster. The curtains are like wedding veils. It's a little girl's dream of life in the fairy palace. The incidental chairs are museum pieces with royal maroon seats. And the rug is pink.

I stared at the dressing table, at the combs and brushes and bottles of perfume. Everything was so neat and orderly that I was afraid to touch anything. The whole place seemed an extension of Gertrude's body.

I opened the drawers of her bureau and felt my way through nightgowns and underwear, searching for God knows what—secret things tucked into secret places. The silk was cool and smooth against my hand. I was a diver in deep seas, plunging into this corner and that and coming up with small embarrassments: a little book on feminine hygiene, a cigarette lighter with strange initials on it, a set of rosary beads. Where were all the love letters? Where was the diary of her secret life? Was it possible that poor Gertrude had no love letters, no secret life?

On my way from Lloyd Harbor to Garden City, I transformed myself from Claude to Marc. In Garden City, I parked the rented Volkswagen at the railroad station and took a taxi to Laura's house. What happened there I cannot yet comment on. Objectivity may be the coward's way out but it's all I can do at the moment. So we are back again in Marc McMann's little theatre and the curtain is about to go up on an absurd scene. I will join you, in silence, in the audience.

(The scene is the Haley house in Garden City, Marc McMann comes to the front door and rings the bell. Through an invisible wall we see Gladys Haley tightening her dressing gown around her as she walks, somewhat unsteadily, towards the door. She is not really drunk but she has been nipping away at something alcoholic for about an hour and a half. There is only one lamp on in the living room. It stands on an end table beside the couch. Under the lamp, there is a book face down. Beside it, is an overflowing ashtray.)

GLADYS : (answering the door) Oh! Marc! How nice. Come in, dear. Come in.

MARC : I know it's late but I thought I'd stop in for a minute, since I happened to be out this way.

GLADYS : (leading him to the couch) We half expected you for dinner but when you didn't show up we figured you were busy or something.

MARC : (looking around) Is Laura here?

GLADYS : She and her father went to the movies. In fact, they just left a few minutes ago. Too bad. You could have gone with them.

MARC : (studying her. She seems to have on nothing more than the dressing gown.) And you were probably getting ready for bed. I'm sorry. I should have called.

GLADYS : Nonsense, Marc. You're practically one of the family. In fact, next week ...

MARC : (frowning) Next week? (does a quick calculation on his fingers) Is today already the 25th?

GLADYS : (taking him by the arm and leaning against him) What's the matter, getting cold feet? (She laughs)

MARC : (Forces a laugh) Funny how time slips away, isn't it?

GLADYS : (She shakes her head.) It's downright scary. You know, it seems just like yesterday that Laura was just a little girl going off to school with her little lunchbox and her books. (Dreamily) A little doll in her bell-like dresses, her hair tied back in a ponytail. (Sighs) And now all of a sudden she's a grown woman and she's getting married. Before you know it I'll be a grandmother.

MARC : Don't rush us; we're not even married yet.

GLADYS : (laughs) How about a drink, Marc? I must confess I was having one myself. I was settling down with a good book, as they say. Only it's not a very good book.

MARC : (picking up the book from the end table) *Portnoy's Complaint?* You shouldn't be reading things like that?

GLADYS : I know it's absolute filth. (Goes out and comes back with two drinks. Marc is sitting on the couch. She sits down beside him. He was thumbing through the book but puts it down to accept the drink.) All that guy can think about is sex and how much he hates his mother. His poor mother. I mean I feel sorry for her. After all, she means well. And then all that you know—all that playing with himself. There's something wrong with the guy, don't you think?

MARC : I thought it was a funny book.

GLADYS : Well, I guess so, in a way. It's pretty funny. I mean, you have to laugh sometimes, but still . . .

MARC : (Still studying Gladys. Drinks. A very slight sinister tone creeps into his voice. He feels his eyelids getting a little heavy. He doesn't know why.) How come you didn't go to the movies with Laura and Homer?

GLADYS : I thought I'd like to be alone for a while. You know, I'm never alone in the evening around here. Even if the kids go out, Homer is here, snoring in front of the TV.

MARC : I don't blame him. TV is pretty boring these days.

GLADYS : Yeah, but Homer finds everything boring. He doesn't read. He doesn't follow sports. He doesn't—well, he doesn't do anything. I'm surprised he went to the movies tonight.

MARC : (Pauses. Drinks) He hasn't lost interest in you, has he?

GLADYS : That's a funny thing for you to say.

MARC : I'm sorry, I thought you said I was practically a member of the family. Besides, I know how it is. I have lots of married friends, some of them in their forties. They all say the same thing.

GLADYS : What do you say?

MARC: (pretending to be embarrassed) Well, you know. It's not that they don't love each other. It's just that physically they get a little bored with each other and before you know it, weeks go by—even months.

GLADYS: (blushing) It's true. But I bet in most cases it's not the woman's fault. It's the husband who gets fat and lazy. Women in their forties are—you know. They reach a...

MARC: (rescuing her) Yes, I know. They have a very strong sexual need. I wonder why that is. Some people think that husbands should be younger than their wives.

GLADYS: It's not a bad idea. (Takes a long drink. Accepts a cigarette from Marc.) I wouldn't mind having a younger husband.

MARC: (coming closer to light her cigarette) You could pass for much younger yourself. I mean, you're a good-looking woman.

GLADYS: (She pokes him playfully) You're just saying that to be nice. (Showing the effects of drinking.) Listen, Marc, I'm almost forty-five. I've had it. I've got a grown daughter who's getting married. I've got a son in college. Before you know it I'll be a grandmother.

MARC: But you haven't even got any grey hair.

GLADYS: (laughs) Are you kidding? I wouldn't dare let it grow out. (She touches her hair, as if to see if it's in place.)

MARC: I thought you were a natural blonde.

GLADYS: Listen, Marc, let me give you a piece of advice. There's nothing natural any more. Don't trust anybody or anything. (Gets up and goes out. Returns with the bottle of Scotch. Pours them both a generous drink over the old ice cubes.)

MARC: Thanks for the motherly advice.

GLADYS: Don't be sarcastic. You sound like Portnoy. Besides, I'm not old enough to be your mother. In fact, you and I are closer in age than you and Laura.

MARC: Does that bother you?

GLADYS: Well, naturally, we all thought about it. I persuaded Homer that it didn't make any difference. But his brother Virgil—well, he didn't like the idea too much.

MARC: I get the impression that Uncle Virgil's not too wild about me anyway.

GLADYS : Oh, that Virgil, he's a jerk. I wouldn't listen to anything he said.

MARC : What exactly did he say?

GLADYS : Oh, nothing.

MARC : Come on, tell me. I mean, there's no generation gap between us or anything. We're practically the same age. What did he say? Did he say I was queer or something?

GLADYS : No, not exactly. Oh, it's too stupid to talk about. There's nothing wrong with you.

MARC : How do you know?

GLADYS : How does any woman know. Instinctively, I guess.

MARC : (raising his voice somewhat) Yeah, but what about Virgil's instinct?

GLADYS : He doesn't have any instinct. He's a jerk.

MARC : And what does your instinct tell you? (Intense and a little angry.)

GLADYS : Now, now, don't get all upset, Marc. (Pats him on the leg.) Virgil is just naturally suspicious. I can remember when he used to think that everybody was a communist.

MARC : And now he thinks everybody's queer.

GLADYS : Well, not everybody.

MARC : Just me!

GLADYS : No, no, you're getting me all confused. We never believed a word he said.

MARC : But you must have some doubts. Accusations always stir up doubts.

GLADYS : Not necessarily, Virgil is always saying dumb things. You should hear what he used to say about Kennedy.

MARC : (slumps dejectedly into the couch and pretends to pout like a little boy.) You can imagine how I felt when Laura told me. I was afraid he would poison your minds against me.

GLADYS : (motherly) Oh, poor Marc. (Puts her arm around his shoulder and kisses him gently on the cheek.) You must have felt awful. We should have said something. We should have reassured you. (Kisses him again.)

MARC : No, I should have reassured *you*.

GLADYS : How?

MARC: I don't know. I should have done something or said something.

GLADYS: But what could you have done? Don't be ridiculous. Besides . . .

MARC: (Turns towards her suddenly, a little drunkenly.) Gladys, would you mind if I kissed you?

GLADYS: What?

MARC: Oh, not that way. Not personally. I just want to reassure you, that's all.

GLADYS: Oh, that's different. I thought for a minute . . .

MARC: (Stops her with a passionate kiss. She struggles stiffly at first but then melts into his arms. After a while, they part.) There. Is that the kiss of a queer? Are you reassured now?

GLADYS: (catching her breath) Yes. No. I mean . . . I don't know. I . . .

MARC: (Kisses her again before she can go on. This time he slips his hand into her dressing gown and fondles her breast. Finally they part again.) There, is that convincing? Do you believe me now? Do you believe that I adore women, that I love to kiss them and touch them and make love to them?

GLADYS: (reduced to mumbling and confusion) I always thought. I mean you always were—that was just fine, I guess.

MARC: I hope I haven't hurt your feelings or anything. I just want you to know. I want you to be absolutely sure. After all, it's your only daughter.

GLADYS: Yes, my only daughter. I understand. Yes, of course. You want to show me. You want me to be sure. (She leans towards him heavily.)

MARC: (Kissing her again and fondling her passionately). You'll have no peace of mind, unless you know for yourself. (In a heavy whisper). And there's only one way to know for yourself, isn't there?

GLADYS: (half swooning) Oh, yes, yes, only one way.

MARC: I could have told you but you might not have believed me, and for the rest of your life you would have wondered. (Her robe is open and Marc allows her to fall back on the couch. He continues to caress her and kiss her. Her eyes are closed and she is drawing him on top of her. He fumbles with his zipper.

GLADYS : Poor Marc, poor boy. Of course, you must show me. Please show me. Come. Come. Don't be afraid. (She draws him frantically on to her.)

MARC : (makes vigorous love to her. She makes incoherent noises and heaves about until she is nearly hysterical. A volcanic spasm catapults her to the floor, where she continues to writhe, unaware apparently of her fall. She gropes blindly for her partner, upsetting the coffee table. Marc picks her up bodily and carries her to her bedroom. She seems to be in the throes of an endless orgasm as he drops her on her bed. She is out of touch with reality.) Are you all right? (She doesn't answer. In her dream world she seems to be riding a wild horse.) I'm sorry. I didn't mean to get carried away. (He shakes her, but fails to wake her. Then he shrugs his shoulders and goes out. In the living room, he finishes his drink in one gulp and puts on his jacket. He adjusts his shirt and tie as best he can and goes out the front door.)

Monday, 26 May

'As far as I'm concerned, Gladys Haley is just another woman with hot pants. I do not feel that any more profound explanation is necessary for what happened last night.' That's what I told the face in my bathroom mirror this morning. The poor bastard looked at me with his tired eyes and his face full of soap. 'But what am I going to tell Popoff?' he said. 'Tell *Pop*off to *fuck*-off,' I said, and mowed a path through the soap.

I walked to the office in the hazy morning, conscious of sidewalks and brick façades, as though I were a character in an art film. It would be unfair of me to say I had premonitions, because I almost always have premonitions. A high level of anxiety, says Popoff. Still, when something actually happens, it makes one wonder about invisible dimensions and psychic powers.

Everything seemed normal at the office. The beehive noises of the corporate machine were as reassuring and as terrifying as ever. One feels that as long as the hum and rattle goes on all will be well. Like kitchen noises downstairs when one is a child in bed in the winter, or eternal crickets in the summer night as one rocks on the back porch. But when the machine stops, when the birds cannot be heard in the morning or the crickets at night, then one knows that something is wrong and that invisible disaster is near.

I had no real clue that anything was wrong until Hinkle came into my cubicle. He was unusually subdued and polite but there was a sinister light in his eye. 'Did you have a nice week-end?' he said.

I was unnecessarily abrupt. 'What do you want?' I said, pretending to be busy.

'We need the Kuntz correspondence file,' he said.

For a moment the words didn't mean anything to me. I stared up at him, at his narrow bespectacled face and at his black tie. Why was he wearing a black tie, I wondered, but I did not ask. Finally, I said, 'What do you need it for?'

'Oh, didn't Linda tell you?' he said.

'Tell me what?' I said. By this time I knew something was happening.

'We've reassigned some of your projects.' he said. 'We've given Kuntz to Miss Workman. I think she'll be able to handle it all right.'

'I don't understand,' I said. 'What's this all about?'

'I really can't say. You'll have to talk to Leonard. Aren't you having lunch with him or something today?' I felt that he was toying with me and I wanted to leap at this throat and throttle him until he pleaded for mercy and stopped his stupid game.

I got up and walked slowly around my desk towards him. He backed away a few steps towards the door. 'Why are you taking Kuntz away from me?' I said.

'I'm sorry, Marc, old boy,' he said. 'Leonard asked me not to discuss it. He said he'd rather talk to you himself.'

'What else have you taken away?' I said.

'Kleinman and Dawson,' he said. 'That's all so far.' He backed away another step. 'You'd better talk to Leonard. He said something about lunch.'

'Who's doing the Dawson now?' I said.

'Well,' he said, 'as a matter of fact I am.'

'You?' I said, the rage accumulating in my throat, so that my voice was half a growl.

'Well, yes,' he said. 'I mean it's an advanced grammar text. Who else could do it? After all, I have a . . .'

'No, no,' I said, interrupting him with a pointed finger and blazing eyes. 'Don't tell me, Harvey. Let me guess. You have a PhD. Right?' I moved towards him again. 'You have a PhD

146

in English from New York University. Right? You wrote your dissertation on the gerund and the participle. Didn't you?' Suddenly I shouted, 'Didn't you?'

He swallowed hard. 'Don't get excited, Marc,' he said. 'Leonard will explain. I don't know what he has in mind. Honest I don't.'

'Bullshit,' I said. 'You know exactly what's in his mind. You've been poisoning his mind against me for months.'

'No, no, Marc,' he said. 'You've got it all wrong. I've been defending you. I've been covering up for you.'

I turned away in disgust and went back to my desk. I sat down heavily and said, 'Hinkle, if you weren't already so pathetic I'd do something nasty to you. Go on, get out of here. Leave me alone.'

He opened the door and started out. But then he turned and said in a matter-of-fact voice, 'Oh did you know that Paul Garrison died last night?'

I looked blankly in his direction but did not say anything. He closed the door quietly and I became conscious once again of office machines and collective voices. But beyond the ordinary noise, there was a buzzing in my ear and a slight ringing which I could not account for and which I could not blot out.

I sat there for a long time without doing anything. I found it hard to focus my attention. If it wasn't for the telephone, I might have stayed that way all day. I recognised Leonard Pike's voice and answered his questions in a dull monotone. He suggested that we go across the street for lunch and I could not refuse.

At twelve-thirty Leonard opened the door to my cubicle, I stood up and straightened my tie. 'I'm ready,' I said. As we went out, I imagined that the beehive was suddenly quiet and that everyone was staring at us but perhaps it was only the lunch-hour lull.

By the time we sat down to lunch, I was quite calm. Leonard, however, was unusually talkative, the only indication that he was somewhat nervous. 'What will you have to drink?' he said.

I felt myself smile grimly. 'I guess a silver bullet would be in order right now,' I said. 'You know, a very dry one.'

He looked down at the white tablecloth. 'Then I guess you know what this is all about,' he said.

I felt suddenly sorry for him. He looked old and weary. There were lines in his lean face and his eyelids kept blinking. 'I suppose so,' I said.

'I'm sorry it's come to this,' he said, 'but I'm afraid you haven't given us much choice.'

'Oh, don't worry about it,' I said. 'I'll survive one way or another.'

'I'm sure you will,' he said. 'And I'll do everything I can to help. I have a lot of friends in the industry and I can honestly give you a good recommendation. You've been a good editor for a long time. It's just recently that something has gone wrong. I wish I knew exactly what it was.'

'Listen, Leonard,' I said, genuine compassion welling up in me, 'I understand. I mean, you've got a job to do and you can't solve everybody's personal problems. Right?'

'Right!' he echoed and fixed his eyes on me for the first time. 'I didn't expect you to take it this way. I don't know whether I feel better or worse about the whole thing.'

'Oh to hell with it,' I said. 'Let's forget it and have a drink. And while we're at it, let's have one for Paul.'

A sad smile spread over his face and he seemed to get smaller and smaller in his chair opposite me. Suddenly I could see in his face, all the ages of his life: the boy, the young man, the father, And through him, as though he were a mirror, I could see all the ages of my own life. I was riding my rocking-horse, I was making love, I was writing a book, I was sipping soup with a sunken, toothless mouth.

I started to laugh, quietly at first, and then more loudly. Leonard looked at me, a little puzzled, as though he didn't know Whether to join me or not. At last he broke down, and a snorting chuckle escaped from him. His eyes brightened. Our faces broadened and the laughter grew, until we were both roaring and wiping our eyes, as though we were both victims of the ultimate joke.

148

Outside Enrico's, I shook hands with Leonard and said I wouldn't be coming back to the office just then. Warmed by two martinis and a little wine, I set out to find a congenial bar where I could have a quiet drink and consider my circumstances.

At the White Horse, I had another martini and decided it was all for the best. That is, having been nudged out of the nest, I might now be more capable of decisive action. But at Sullivan's Dostoevskyan despair began to creep in. What if my master-plan failed? Would I ever really be able to find another job? At the San Remo, I met a kid with long hair and we talked about silence. He said there were a lot of different kinds of it. He drew me a picture of one kind. It looked like fornicating flies. I told him so and he said, 'Exactly!' I bought him another glass of wine and staggered down to another place on Bleeker Street.

By four-thirty I was too drunk to tackle the problem at the philosophical level and I found my thoughts getting repetitious. I would get a gun, I thought. I would get a gun and go there. I would go there and I would kill her. I would kill her and that would be that. Yes, that would be that. It was simple. It was really very simple. Much simpler than Popoff could ever imagine. Popoff! I squinted to focus on my watch. Popoff! I had forgotten all about him. I felt it was urgent that I make my appointment. There were things that I had to say to him, things that I had to settle with him. It was important.

When it was my turn to see my mental dentist, I marched in boldly and sat down heavily in the black leather chair. 'I want you to know, Sir, that I'm drunk,' I said rather proudly.

'Obviously,' he said. In his voice, I could detect that typically Jewish intolerance of the Christian drinker.

'Are you annoyed?' I said.

'Did you come here drunk to annoy me?' he said, as cunning as ever :

'No,' I said. 'I came here to tell you that there's more therapy in booze, dollar for dollar, than in psychoanalysis.'

'Tell me,' he said, 'was there a special occasion for this—this indulgence today?'

'You mean why am I drunk?' I said. 'Well, if you mean why am I drunk, why the hell don't you say, "Why are you drunk?" Why all this—this' (I searched with my hand for the right word), 'this euphemistic shit?'

'All right,' he said quietly. 'Why are you drunk?'

'Well,' I said, 'it's a natural human condition that follows hot on the heels of having imbibed an excess of beverages with high alcoholic content. How about that for circumlocution?'

He didn't laugh and he didn't say anything.

'All right, so it's not very funny,' I said. 'I'll tell you why I got drunk. I got drunk because I lost my job, and that is the traditional thing to do. I am a very traditional fellow, a good American, a puritan sort of, and when I was a kid I saw too many movies.'

'Oh, I'm sorry to hear about your job,' he said. 'You must be very upset.'

'Not especially,' I said. 'I was about to quit anyway. You see I am on the brink of a great break-through, after which my life will be entirely different!'

'Oh?' he said, sounding intensely interested. Out of the corner of my eye I saw him lean forward. 'Would you like to tell me about it?'

I shook my head, 'No,' I said, 'I don't want to tell you about it. I don't want to tell you about anything any more. I hate to tell you this, Dr. Popoff, but I don't have any faith in you or your mental magic. And besides, now that I've lost my job I can't afford you.'

'I think this is the wrong time for you to quit,' he said. 'I can wait for the money. That needn't worry you.'

'I feel there is a more direct solution to my problem,' I said, 'but I don't want to talk about it. The trouble with analysis is that it makes Hamlets of us all. We brood and never act. Almost any clear decision is better than indecision.'

'But if there is a conflict there can be no clear decision,' he said.

'Ah, but you remember the Gordian knot,' I said. ' "One might spend a lifetime trying to untie it" but not I, Sir, not I. Like Alexander, I will cut right through the bloody thing.'

'I hope you are not thinking of anything reckless,' he said.

'Reckless?' I said. 'I am not the reckless type. No, I am quite conservative, quite meticulous. Don't worry, whatever I do will be done well.'

'I hope so,' he said.

He started to say something else but I wasn't listening. I got up and came over to his desk with an extended hand. 'I'm sorry that it has to end this way,' I said, and it occurred to me that I sounded as though I were referring to a love affair. We shook hands. 'It's nothing personal.'

'If you need me,' he said, 'you can call me any time, either here or at home.' Our eyes met, possibly for the first time since my visits began. I thought he looked tired and concerned. I wanted to apologise for having been mean to him and for having arrived drunk but all I did was nod and go out.

On the sidewalk, in the bright afternoon, I felt alone and confused. I started to walk without knowing where exactly I was going. And then, impulsively, to ward off the grip of panic, I hailed a taxi and told him to take me to the Saxon Arms Hotel.

I changed in the men's room of a busy cafeteria in the neighbourhood, and emerged as Claude Elmath. Instantly, I felt relieved. Even the effects of the booze seemed diminished, as though Claude had a greater capacity than Marc. I went to my room and rested for a while, forcing myself to think about the whole situation. I decided, finally, that everything was all right. I would call Laura later and tell her that I had to take an urgent business trip to Chicago. Then I would concentrate on locating a gun that could not be traced. By Sunday, everything should be ready. I would make sure that there was no trace of Marc at the Saxon Arms and no trace of Claude at my apartment. I would also have to visit my mother once more to make sure that she suspected nothing. What else? What else? I would have to clear out of my office eventually. What should I do with the gun afterwards? There must be no fingerprints on it. Perhaps I should bury it.

Tuesday, 27 May

I didn't get out of bed until mid-morning. I seemed to be avoiding the crucial problem of how to get hold of an untraceable gun.

It was strange not to go to work on an ordinary Tuesday. I felt rather lost sitting there on the edge of the bed at the Saxon Arms. I had the vague feeling that I should make some telephone calls or write some letters. Finally, I forced myself to shower and shave, after which I felt considerably more capable of action. I put on my disguise and went out for breakfast.

During the course of the day I thought a lot about guns and managed to see a few. I began, rather pointlessly, by inquiring about a pair of duelling pistols in the window of an antique shop. I was impressed by the workmanship and my imagination carried me back two hundred years to a misty morning on the outskirts of Paris, where I faced—who? The Marquis de Sade perhaps. Funereal cloaks, broad-brimmed hats, horses steaming, the ground soft with spring rain, the weapons heavy in our hands. My heart pounded as I paced slowly away from my enemy. 'They can be mounted on a plaque, of course,' said the antique dealer, dropping a boulder into the clear pond of my mind and killing everybody. I pointed the gun at him playfully and he stepped aside with the polite smile of a man who accepts the essential madness of all mankind. I said I would have to think about it and his smile tightened and shrivelled until his mouth, contracted between heavy cheeks, looked like the wrong end of his anatomy.

In a sporting goods store, I inquired about shotguns. I assumed there would be less legal difficulty about buying a gun for hunting than a pistol. The shotgun struck me as cumbersome for my purposes. I couldn't very well arrive gun in hand without arousing some suspicion. She might see me from the window and lock the door. I might explain, of course, that I was fond of hunting. Still, it was an awkward weapon to handle at close quarters.

I came back to Sammy's for a drink and talked about violence, crime and guns with Henry the bartender. I asked him if he had ever been held up and he told me in detail about the time two black guys came into the bar and made everyone lie down on the floor. 'But it will never happen again,' he said, producing from somewhere under the bar a .38 calibre revolver. That was it, I thought. That was exactly what I needed. I looked longingly at it, as a child might look at a hopelessly expensive toy in a shop window.

I went back to my room to think about the situation. There were several possibilities. Hadn't I read, for instance, about pawn shops where one could buy a gun with no questions asked? Or had all that changed now after the wave of assassinations? And what about the mail-order arsenals? What was it one could order? Machine-guns, bazookas, mortars, land mines, tanks, howitzers, obsolete atom bombs. All to be used, of course, for purely agricultural purposes. I considered taking a trip out of state but to which state should I go?

My mind kept drifting back to the gun under the bar at Sammy's. If we were alone, I could conceivably distract Henry long enough to steal it. It was a dangerous but interesting plan. It was an adventure in itself that excited me.

I went down to the bar and had a drink. There were two other men there, talking quietly. They both had grey suits. They might have been twins. Henry was smoking and reading the paper. He's a square man with broad shoulders and a round face. All that remains of his hair is a few strands that he lays across a dome of skin. He looks Italian and somewhat more beligerent than he really is.

I studied the situation. The bar is about twenty feet long. If I sat at the very end, it would mean ten feet each way and time to locate the gun. I did not see where he concealed it but I remember the exact spot along the bar. The big problem was to be alone with Henry at precisely the moment when he was forced to step away for a minute. There is a room to the left of the bar into which he occasionally disappears. There is also a trap door that leads into a cellar. I have seen him go down and come back with bottles.

After a while, the two men in grey left and Henry and I were alone. I ordered another Scotch and soda and lit a cigarette. 'Pretty quiet this afternoon,' I said as he set the drink down on a white square of cardboard.

'It'll pick up in about half an hour,' he said. I offered him a cigarette, which he refused. 'But Tuesdays are generally slow.'

'You put in some pretty long hours,' I said.

He shrugged, 'It's the only way with a bar. If I hire another man, he'll cost me a couple hundred a week.'

'Then it's your own place?' I said. My hand trembled slightly as I lifted my glass and he looked towards the sound the ice-cubes made.

'Oh yeah,' he said.

'And what about Sammy?' I said.

He smiled, 'Oh, he's dead. Yeah, he died five years ago, right here behind the bar. Just dropped dead. I bought the place from his wife Rose. We knew them from the old days in Brooklyn. Nice guy Sammy but he drank a hell of a lot. Can't run a bar and drink. You know what I mean? What the hell, you spend twelve hours here, you could drink yourself to death.'

I couldn't think of what to say. I glanced at the bottles against the mirror and then at the clock. The second hand seemed to be moving too fast. It was four thirty-five. Henry yawned and folded his arms across his chest. His shirt sleeves were rolled up and his forearms looked very strong. I kept expecting someone to come in, but nothing happened. My heart pounded, and, in spite of the fact that I was drinking, my mouth felt dry.

I searched frantically for a way to get him away from the bar for a few minutes. If only he had something in the cellar that he did not have at the bar, I could ask for it. 'Listen,' I said. 'What's the best champagne you've got?'

'What do you like?' he said. 'I got some Piper-Heidseck. I got some Moet Chandon.'

'I'm coming back with a lady later who loves champagne,' I said. 'Could you show me a couple of bottles now, so you can put one on ice for me?'

'Sure,' he said, 'but it's going to cost you. What's wrong with the New York State? Hell of a lot cheaper.'

'No, this is something special,' I said. 'Her birthday.'

'Oh,' he said, unimpressed. He moved slowly towards the other end of the bar, hesitated, and then bent down to lift up the trap door.

As soon as he was out of sight, I went around the bar and looked for the gun. In the clutter that confronted me I couldn't seem to get my bearings. There were glasses and drainboards and coasters and sliced lemons. I was close to panic when I saw a narrow drawer under the work counter. I slid it open and found the gun. It was lying there like a dormant animal.

I stuffed the cold metal weapon into my pocket just as I heard the front door open. A man with a red, glistening face came in and nodded. My feet seemed nailed to the floor. He came up to me and said, 'Gin and tonic!' I felt myself blush violently and thought a blood vessel might explode. I smiled idiotically at him and went back to my seat. 'Henry will be up in a minute,' I said. He looked embarrassed and said, 'Sorry!' He climbed on to a stool and we pretended to ignore one another.

Henry came up with three dusty bottles and put them on the bar. 'I don't get much call for this stuff,' he said. He turned to his other customer and I could hear the man say, 'Gin and tonic.' We glanced at one another and he smiled weakly.

I studied the labels blankly. They didn't mean much to me but I made a choice and Henry said, 'Yeah, I think you can't go wrong with that,' and took all the bottles away.

I had one more drink and tried to collect myself enough to make it to the door without passing out.

Back at my apartment, I put on some water for tea. I put the gun down on the table and stared at it for a while, as though I were expecting it to move. It didn't. I picked it up and, after some fumbling, opened the chamber. It was fully loaded. I took a bullet out, looked at it and inserted it again. I suddenly felt very important.

I took my tea and my gun into the bathroom and took off all my clothes. I soaked in very hot water and sipped tea. The gun was on the closed lid of the toilet and sweated in the humid air. I was fascinated by it. I relaxed into a pleasant haze and my mind began to drift but I could not take my eyes off the gun. I remembered a holster I had as a boy that hung convincingly at the hip and was tied securely around my thigh. It changed my way of walking and the expression on my face.

My body was buoyant in the full tub. I finished my tea and allowed myself to slip in deeper until the water covered my chest. I could hear myself breathing. The warmth stirred me sexually and my erection was like a slow-motion serpent from the sea. It throbbed visibly. My pubic hair was a collar of seaweed. I studied the wet phallic form, lifting my hips somewhat to extend it further into the air. Waves washed away from me as though I were a rising island. How perfectly suited it was, I thought, for its function—the gunman of the life-force. Shoot 'em alive, not dead. Fill 'em with the hot bullet-juice of life. Make love! Make war!

I saw dimly the lethal piece of iron only a few feet from me. Death was that close. Only a few feet away. Only a few seconds. But it was life I had in my hand, the living gun of life. I watched it spit its defiant sperm into the killing air and water. How strong! How brave! Nature's little suicide squadron, blasting away blindly at death, earning glory and honour and love, because their cause is just and their hearts are pure.

I watched the dead heroes slide into the sea. Collectively they were a yellowish ooze, like mucus. But what were they really? What were they under the giant microscope of God's piercing eye? Each sperm an individual, each propelled by a force it obeyed without understanding. Good soldiers, good obedient soldiers of the Great Mother.

I mourned their deaths, each and every one of them, and then washed them vigorously away, because I could not stand being covered with corpses. Then I opened the drain and let the water out—burial at sea. The full circle.

In the living room, wrapped only in a large white towel, I watched the Six o'clock Report on television and considered the problem of Claude's date for the evening, that lady for whom he had ordered the champagne. It seemed to me he had very little choice. The only woman he knew was poor old Nancy McGuire and she was hardly the expensive French champagne type. On the other hand, there was hardly time enough to make a new acquaintance. Of course, he could invent an excuse and show up alone but especially if he had found his gun missing, almost anything might arouse Henry's suspicion.

I was absorbed with the problem when the telephone rang. Instantly and instinctively I knew it must be my mother. She had probably called me at the office and been told—God knows what. But no sooner did that thought, like Jack, fall down, than Jill came tumbling after in the form of another thought. Gertrude was another woman in Claude's brief life.

I picked up the phone, trembling with old fear and new excitement. 'Marc, dear, are you all right?' she said in an overly loud voice, not far from her scolding tone. 'What's wrong? What's going on?'

'Nothing's wrong,' I said. 'I'm perfectly all right.'

'When I called your office today your secretary told me that she did not know when you would be in again. She sounded very mysterious. I don't understand.'

I could imagine the pained expression on her face, that look of cosmetic persecution, as if to say, There are malevolent forces at work in the universe that have chosen me as a special victim. 'There's no great mystery,' I said. 'We've had a disagreement, and—and I've taken some time off.'

'What do you mean?' she said. 'What kind of a disagreement? You haven't lost your job, have you?'

There was a brief silence, after which I said meekly, 'Yes, I think I have.'

She was indignant. 'What? After all these years? Why that's incredible, Marc. What happened? I want to know exactly what happened. We can't let them get away with this.'

'Nothing much happened,' I said. 'I fell behind in my work and Hinkle, the head of the English text division, was down on me. He never liked me much anyway and used any excuse to attack me.'

'But Marc,' she said, 'I don't understand how you could fall behind in your work. You never did before. Perhaps you've been seeing too much of that girl.'

'Please, Gertrude,' I said, 'I'd rather not discuss it right now.'

'I warned you about her, Marc,' she went on. 'I told you she's too young for you. You should find someone your own age, a young widow perhaps.'

'Mother, this had nothing to do with Laura,' I said.

'It most certainly does,' she said, her voice stiff with outrage. 'You've been acting very strangely ever since that girl came into your life. You just haven't been yourself.'

Suppressed laughter was added to my suppressed rage and I was afraid that I could not contain either for very long. In a boyish voice I said, 'I'm all right.'

'What do you mean you're all right?' she said. 'How can you say that when you are jobless, practically destitute and about to assume the responsibilities of a wife and family. God, I don't know how I can stand all this. And, on top of everything else, your poor cousin Emily's in the hospital.'

I wasn't really surprised and I was strangely unmoved, as though she was talking about a stranger, but I said, 'That's terrible. What's wrong with her?'

'She was dragged out of the river by a policeman at three o'clock in the morning,' said Gertrude, emphasising the time as though there was something inherently immoral about three a.m. 'She had been beaten up beforehand.'

'Good Lord,' I said. 'What happened?'

'We don't know,' she said. 'Emily insists she fell in, but that seems unlikely. My guess is that she tried to kill herself.'

'But why?' I said.

'Who knows why,' said Gertrude. 'I'll never understand you or your cousin or your whole generation. In any case, the little idiot should be all right in a few days, so don't worry.'

I wanted to assure her that I wasn't worried but I said nothing. After an awkward pause, Gertrude said, 'I'm more concerned about you than about her. After all, she's a lost soul already. But you, Marc, you have so much—intelligence, good looks, education. You came from a good family. How can you ruin your life like this? No, no don't try to explain over the phone. I know it's complicated. Believe me, Marc, I try to understand. I try to be sympathetic. It's been such a long time since we've had a good talk. Please come and see me. Come tomorrow. I really must see you, Marc. I feel just awful—helpless and awful, with all these terrible things happening. Come for lunch or dinner, whichever you prefer. Now that you're unemployed, I shouldn't think it would matter much.'

'It doesn't,' I said coldly.

'All right, then, *lunch*,' she said. 'At one o'clock.'

'All right,' I said, 'if you insist.'

'I insist,' she said.

'I'll see you tomorrow, then,' I said and hung up without adding a goodbye.

I searched for a cigarette but could find only empty packs in the living room. I looked in the kitchen, but the carton was empty. With increasing irritation, I went through drawers and jacket pockets. At last, I remembered the bathroom. There I found a half-filled pack. As I stooped to pick it up from beside the tub, I saw the gun on the toilet lid. It detonated the obvious chain-reaction of associations: champagne, lady friend, Henry, Claude, Gertrude.

It was getting late. I composed myself for a moment or two and went to the telephone. Carefully I dialled Gertrude's number. The dial returned after each number with its quiet mechanical sound, reminding me of things inexorable, like clocks ticking or heels clicking in prison corridors on the morning of an execution. I had to shut my eyes to imagine myself as Claude. By the time Gertrude answered I was able to use the proper voice. 'This is Claude Elmath,' I said. 'I'm terribly sorry to bother you, but there are a few things I would like to discuss with you before Sunday.'

'Oh, it's no bother at all,' she said with mechanical cheerfulness. Her recovery from despair was disgustingly swift, I thought. 'In fact, I'm rather glad you called.'

'Unlike you Americans, I am awful on the telephone,' I said. 'Couldn't we possibly speak in person?'

'Of course,' she said. 'Would you like to come up this evening?'

I hesitated, unprepared for her invitation. Finally, I said, 'I hope you won't think me overly bold but I've ordered a bottle of champagne to celebrate my first employment in America and it would give me a great pleasure—I mean would you consider sharing it with me while we talk?'

I waited while she considered the matter. 'Well, I don't know,' she said.

'Nothing fancy,' I said. 'Just a little pub around the corner.'

'I suppose so,' she said. 'Yes. Yes, that would be very nice.'

I gave her directions and hung up.

I lit another cigarette and wondered whether or not I had aroused her suspicion in any way. I decided that I had not and prepared myself for an amusing encounter.

At Sammy's, we sat at a small table that Henry reserved for us. On the table, was a candle and a single flower in a narrow vase. It was clear that Henry had not yet missed his gun and therefore, had no reason to suspect me. And after my bold return to the scene, it was not likely that he ever would. I was relieved. I smiled across the table at Gertrude and poured the champagne. After a while Henry came over again. 'Is everything all right?' he said, laying a friendly hand on my shoulder and giving me a man-to-man wink.

'Just fine,' I said. 'Perfect.'

'If there's anything you want, just holler,' he said, and went away.

Gertrude frowned, but I smiled and said, 'He's a colourful character, don't you think?'

She forced herself to agree and we raised our glasses in a toast. 'To you, Mrs. McMann,' I said, 'for helping me to find myself in this strange land.'

She nodded coyly and sipped at her drink. 'Actually, the good fortune is mine for having found someone so competent.'

'I hope I won't disappoint you,' I said.

'Oh, I'm sure you won't,' she said.

We smiled a great deal and said trivial things. I made up questions about tools and trees and septic tanks, which she answered with the pride and precision of a woman who knew and loved her house. The candle flickered, the champagne bubbled, our voices grew soft. 'You might as well call me Gertrude,' she said. 'We'll be seeing a lot of each other.'

'Whatever you say, Mrs. McMann—Gertrude,' I said, and pretended to blush at the intimacy.

'Actually, it's a horrible name and I hate it,' she said, 'but it's the only one I've got.'

'On the contrary,' I said, 'I think it's a lovely name. I have a marvellous aunt named Gertrude.'

Before our little celebration was over, she told me about the death of her poor husband and actually produced a tear or two. I reached across the table and patted her hand comfortingly. She smiled bravely and glanced at her watch. 'Oh my, it's later than I thought,' she said, 'I really must go.'

I was sure that she either wanted me to stop her or to go with her but I had had enough for one day. I paid the bill and we went outside. It was dark, but the city was ablaze with lights.

I offered her my arm and we walked slowly to the corner. 'I'll get you a taxi,' I said.

She said nothing for a moment and then in a tone that was terrifyingly predatory she said, 'You must be hungry. Let me offer you a little supper.'

The hair literally rose under my wig and my scalp began to shrink. I swallowed hard and desperately tried to locate my voice and my wits.

'That's very kind of you,' I said, 'but I'm afraid I can't.'

'Oh?' she said. 'Why not?'

'I'm afraid I'm expected somewhere else,' I said.

Cat-like calculation animated her face and was followed by raised eye-brows and resignation. 'Well, in that case, you have no choice, do you?'

We exchanged pleasant looks of distrust and I hailed her a taxi. We shook hands and said good night. 'Until Sunday,' I said, and she went off with a stiff wave of her gloved hand.

Wednesday, 28 May

I woke up early this morning with the strong urge to clean things up and organise my life. The first thing I had to do was to find a good hiding place for the gun. But I could think of nothing more imaginative than shoving it under the mattress of my bed. Then I washed some dishes and vacuumed the rug. I took the laundry to the laundremat and picked up a few groceries.

By noon, I was able to sit down with a drink and make a list of the things I had to do before Sunday. I had to see my mother, call Laura, pick up our tickets for the trip to Bermuda, get some travellers' cheques, clean out my desk at the office, rent a car, make sure that all my clothes were ready for the wedding, pack a bag for the trip, pay a few bills, send a note to Paul Garrison's wife, and check out of the Saxon Arms.

As I rode up in the elevator to confront my mother in my own persona, I urged myself to be cool, firm, and brief. When she answered the door, she was serious and pale and looked as though she might have been crying. She wore a black dress with a single strand of pearls, as though she had just come from a funeral. She held up her cheek to be kissed and I responded with a dry peck, catching the fragrance of soap and perfume. We managed to avoid the larger issues for about ten minutes but finally Gertrude said, 'Well, you certainly have gotten yourself into an awful mess, haven't you?'

'It's not so awful,' I said.

'Not so awful?' she echoed. 'I don't see how you can say that. You're entering into a disastrous marriage, your career is ruined and you're alienating yourself from me. And what's more you look just terrible. What have you been doing with yourself? Have you been drinking?'

'A little,' I said.

She shook her head and tried to look compassionate. 'Marc, my dear,' she said, 'what's happened to your judgment? You used to be so sensible.'

I looked into my salad as though into the sea from which most of the ingredients had come. 'I'll be all right,' I said quietly.

'And what do you plan to do for money?' she said.

'I'll find another job,' I said.

'But it's not that simple,' she said. 'Why should anyone give you a job? I mean, you haven't exactly distinguished yourself, have you?'

I considered the question and shrugged my shoulders. 'No, I don't suppose I have,' I said. 'But don't worry.'

'But I *do* worry,' she said. 'I don't want to see you unhappy.' She put her fork down and dabbed at her mouth with her napkin. 'Look, dear,' she said, 'I have an offer to make you, a final offer. I hope you won't take it the wrong way. I can be very generous about some things and very stubborn about other things.'

'I'm not interested in your offers,' I said.

'Oh, I think this one will interest you all right,' she said. Her smile was sinister. She caught my stare and held me with her eyes. I dared not look away. 'You say you want to be a writer. Well, I will give you a chance to be a writer. I will give you the caretaker's cottage outright and seven thousand a year for the next five years. And, of course, you will continue as heir and beneficiary.'

'You mean if I don't marry Laura,' I said.

'Naturally,' she said. 'You can live there in comfort and work with a free mind. You're a very creative person. I'm sure you will succeed one day.'

'But what about the man you've hired?' I said. 'Haven't you promised him the cottage?'

She narrowed her cat's eyes and looked at me as though I were a mouse. 'If you come to Lloyd Harbor, we won't need him, will we?'

I felt suddenly very weary and far out at sea. I wanted to close my eyes and drown and be done with it. But something in me—rage or hope or fear—made me cry out to her and the heaving waves, 'No! No! No! I won't do it.'

She threw her napkin down and pushed back her chair. She walked away from the table and stood for a few moments at the window with her back to me.

I didn't know what to say. I stood up and walked towards her. As I was about to put my hand on her shoulder, she turned suddenly and in the same motion slapped me as hard as she could across the face. 'Why can't you ever do the right thing?' she said furiously.

I had an impulse to shove her through the window. But at the same time I had an urge to run away. She seemed formidable as she stood there, wounded and angry. I felt small and weak, like a child.

'You'd better go,' she said. 'I think we have nothing more to say to one another.'

I made an incoherent sound that might have been an apology or a moan and then turned quickly away from her and went to the front door. She did not try to stop me.

Back at the apartment, I went directly to the bedroom and felt under the mattress for the gun. When I didn't find it instantly, I began to panic but then it was there, hard and cold and heavy in my hand. I studied it, turning it over and around, opening and closing the chamber, putting the safety on and off. Then I removed all the bullets and pulled the trigger. I needed practice. I had never fired a gun in my life. I turned on the television set and used the characters in a soapbox opera as targets.

I looked for other targets. I went to the window and picked off four pedestrians. They went on their way, unaware that they were dead. I aimed at windows across the way but there was no one there. The geraniums on my lady's windowsill were very red in the afternoon sun.

When there was no one else to kill, I put the gun to my head and squeezed the trigger. Click, I was dead. If I had a soul, would it come out of my mouth and go to heaven as in those medieval drawings?

I tried to think about what had to be done next but I could not focus clearly on the problem. I felt my heart. It was beating slowly. I took my pulse. It was only fifty. How was that possible? I took it again. It was the same. Perhaps something was wrong. Perhaps it was about to stop altogether. I felt the injection of fear circulate in my blood. My heart paused and then galloped. I leapt up from the couch and threw the gun down on the coffee table. My hands were trembling and I couldn't quite catch my breath.

I lay down for a while and eventually dozed. I woke up in time for the seven o'clock news. I had tuna fish, baked beans and a bottle of beer. I was unusually hungry. After my makeshift dinner I had a strong desire for something sweet. I could find nothing in the house, so I decided to walk down to Eighth Street to look for something.

The early evening world was a technicolor reality. I was hypersensitive to everything, every face, every red vest or blue shirt or glittering piece of costume jewelry. I felt the brittleness of glass window panes in the shops. I felt the concrete hardness of the sidewalk. Signs winked at me and the traffic that passed was a nightmare of real machines. Their fumes poisoned me. Their horns blasted me. Their motors roared in my guts. There was a sudden rushing sound in my ears again, as of waterfalls.

I stopped in a delicatessen and looked around for something to satisfy my itchy mouth, my craving blood. The riot of boxes and tins, the shelves of canned, packaged, frozen, smoked and preserved foods filled me with excitement. The excitement was partly a vibration in my head and partly a sexual vibration. There were giant chocolate bars and cookies and packaged cakes. There were jars of hard candy and all those marshmallow and caramel things—Mars Bars, Baby Ruths, and Milky Ways. There were Goobers and Jujubs, Good and Plenty, Chiclets, Chunkies and Chocolate Babies. I was hurled back into childhood. Oh, the Chocolate Babies and the Tootsie Rolls, the bubble gum of yesteryear! I could taste it. I could remember picking it from my upper lip when the bubble burst—almost thirty years ago. Incredible! How utterly incredible the passage of time is. How incredible life is. The buzzing of intelligent flies. Self-conscious insects, good for a day perhaps, one long summer day. The sun oozes across the sky. We race through infancy, youth, maturity, middle age. In the late afternoon, the sun swells and deepens and falls more swiftly, as though it is heavier and rushes to rest behind the horizon. Old age is upon us. Fat and black and feeble, we batter ourselves against invisible window panes to follow the dying light. And then it is over and we lie upside down in stiff silence, waiting to be buried by spiders.

'Can I help you?' came a voice from behind the cheeses, pickles and potato salad.

Oh, Christ, yes. I thought. Help me! Help me! 'Peanut brittle,' I said. It was a sudden inspiration. It was exactly what I wanted. Somehow it would make all the difference.

'Right behind you,' said the bald-headed apron.

I turned and saw two diminutive girls. They were dressed like little Indians with headbands and beads and tunics and they seemed to be amused by the fig newtons they held in their hands. At first I thought they were very small children, but then I could see that they were at least in their teens. They both had dark hair that fell short of their shoulders, and round little faces with features like cut-out dolls.

I took them home. It wasn't very difficult. I gave them wine. I played with them. Perhaps they were sent by God. Perhaps they were meant to be a sign . . . but of what?

I must have gotten drunk. I was pouring wine on them and licking it up. Did I make love to them? *Love!* Good Lord what a stupid expression. No, I didn't make love to them—I gored them, I killed them. No, I didn't kill them. Perhaps I should have.

Thursday, 29 May

I stayed in bed all day and considered my circumstances. There is a great deal to consider and it is all very difficult. I live these days in a strange fog, through which I catch an occasional patch of clear sky. But I am essentially a logical person and capable of careful analysis. I know that, given enough time, I will be able to understand almost anything.

I brought a pot of coffee to the table beside my bed, propped myself up on one elbow and forced myself to concentrate in a systematic way. I came to the following conclusions:

(1) Life is absurd, but, nevertheless, worth living, because death is not only absurd, but ridiculous. (2) I am a hypersensitive person, which sharpens my sense of reality. This accounts for both my intense fear and my intense pleasure. (3) I am essentially an artist, which means that I am obsessed with the need to bring order out of chaos. I must write my novel. (4) The only order that is possible is internal order. External order is a utopian dream that will never be realised. I mean the world will never achieve its utopia. The world may, in fact, end shortly, and it doesn't matter. (5) I am justifiably selfish. (6) My mother is an emotional failure who is trying to use me. She feeds on me. She castrates me. She destroys me. She is a ruthless liar and an incestuous whore. (7) Emily is a masochist and a nymphomaniac. (8) Uncle Phil is about to be stabbed from behind his curtain—not by me, but by his former mistress, his brother's wife. (9) I am a sexual desperado because sex is nature's answer to death. I am the hanged man with the uncontrollable orgasm. (10) I must not

167

squander myself in pointless adventures. (11) I need long periods of solitude and serenity. I should live in the country. (12) Laura will provide me with stability, love and sanity. This is the only way I can come to terms with life. (13) Life must be simple in every sense. I must avoid confusion. (14) I would like to be immortal but I will settle for a long, rich life and a little real wisdom at the end, or at least comfortable senility to cushion the final blow. (15) 'Ripeness is all.'

I stayed in bed for almost twenty-four hours, dozing intermittently. Then I opened a can of peanuts, poured myself a drink and watched an old movie on television. I had a delicious sense of comfort as I followed the familiar actors through the familiar plot. For a short time, I lived in a well-ordered world where I could be sure that evil would be punished and good would ultimately be triumphant.

Friday, 30 May

I have been 'out of town' all week. Not only as far as Laura is concerned, but in another sense. The days of this week have run together, as they do on holidays. But now the holiday is over and I must apply myself to urgent business. This has been a long intermission before the last act. And now the curtain is about to go up.

This morning, I went up to the Saxon Arms as Claude. I paid my bill and checked out. I could not take the chance of leaving anything behind, lest, through their science and cunning, the police find a link between Marc and Claude. I wiped away fingerprints from anything I might have touched and checked the bureau and bathroom for stray hairs.

I had lunch alone in a restaurant on Forty-first Street and drank a whole bottle of wine. I emerged into the sunlight again, drowsy and a little subdued. I transformed myself in the New York Public Library and as Marc McMann, headed for my apartment.

When I got home, I called Laura, who scolded me for not calling her every day from Chicago. She poured a dozen trivial things into my ear and I listened patiently. I said I couldn't come out tonight because I had just gotten in and was very tired but that I would be out first thing in the morning and we would spend a quiet day at the beach or in the country. She offered to pack a picnic and I kissed her for her sweetness.

I wandered around for a few hours but couldn't make a connection. I wound up sitting in the park staring towards the fountain. The benches were full. The air reeked with loneliness and sex. I wanted to leap up and announce a public orgy but I only sat there, as helpless and distracted as all the others. A black fag went by, bloodshot eyes scanning us. I looked away.

Later I waited up for my nurses to come home but when they did they had two young men with them. I was furious. I could have killed them all. I took off all my clothes, pulled open my blinds and presented myself to the dark and benignly indifferent universe.

Saturday, 31 May

I got up early and drove to Garden City to see Laura. She greeted me with flower-like freshness, her hair soft and black against a very white sweater and abbreviated skirt. I had almost forgotten how young and beautiful she was. I felt soiled beside her. 'Where's your mother?' I said.

'Oh, she decided to stay in bed,' she said. 'She's not feeling very well.'

'Is she sick?' I said.

'Oh no,' she said. 'Just the usual kind of thing. She's only forty-five, you know.' I found the remark a little sickening. The usual kind of thing!

We did not linger in the house very long. We collected the lunch and got into the car without knowing exactly where we were going. We headed east, considering the Hamptons or possibly the North Fork or Shelter Island.

As we approached Route 110 on the Expressway I pulled into the exit lane. 'Where are we going?' said Laura.

'I thought you'd like to see the house in Lloyd Harbor before my mother disowns me,' I said.

'Oh, I'd love to, ' she said. 'I like houses anyway.' And we drove on.

Entering the house with Laura was an odd experience. She so obviously didn't belong there that she seemed for a moment a stranger even to me. I took her on the same tour we used to provide for new visitors in the old days—first the downstairs area : the living room, the dining room across the centre hall, the old-fashioned kitchen, the sun porch and patio, the library; then the upstairs with its half a dozen bedrooms, most of them unused since my father died. 'Oh, I just love it,' Laura kept saying. 'It's just a darling house and so beautifully decorated. I'll give your mother credit for that.'

'Yes,' I said blankly. 'She has good taste.'

We went outside and I showed her how far the property extended and then took her down to the caretaker's cottage. 'Oh, it's too perfect,' she said as we approached along the slate path. 'And this was supposed to be your studio, wasn't it?'

'Yes,' I said, taking the key out of my pocket, and then a strange thing happened. I looked at the old key and I looked at the cottage. I saw Laura standing beside the locked door, her whiteness against the whiteness of the door all bathed in dazzling sunlight, with violently red roses climbing a trellis beyond the first shuttered window and the shimmering green trees in the distance down the sloping lawn. I was paralysed by a sudden panic that actually made me dizzy and must have showed in my face. Laura's smile faded into a frown. 'What's wrong?' she said, putting her hand on my arm.

'Nothing,' I said. 'It's—it's getting late. We'd better go.'

'But I want to see your cottage,' she said.

'It's nothing special,' I said. 'Just an ordinary little place.'

'But it won't take long,' she insisted. 'Just let me look inside.'

Before I knew what was happening, she took the key out of my hand and opened the door. I wanted to leap on her from behind and strangle her. How easy it would be, I thought, and a whole series of events shot through my mind. I saw myself snapping her delicate neck and dragging her body towards the woods. I imagined the careful grave I would dig for her and the first shovelful of dirt on her young face and white sweater.

She disappeared into the cool interior of the house and I followed her, still in the grip of my murderous impulses. I heard her girlish voice through a haze as she marvelled at the place. I was afraid that I would lose control and do something against my own will. It was the same feeling I had when I stood in high places and looked down.

Fortunately, she went into another room. I did not follow her. I stood by the fireplace and lit a cigarette. In a moment or two the mood passed and I felt better, except for the pounding of my heart.

When she reappeared she had a meditative look. 'I'm sorry, honey,' she said. 'It must be difficult for you to look at this place. I should have realised.'

'It's all right,' I said.

'Well, don't worry,' she said. 'Maybe one day your mother will change her mind. In fact, maybe it's all a bluff; maybe she won't change her will after all. And maybe eventually she'll let us live here.'

I smiled wisely. 'You don't know my mother,' I said.

We locked up the cottage and then the big house and went on our way. A couple of hours later we were in Easthampton, sunning ourselves on the beach and eating cold chicken. Laura insisted that we walk down the beach to an isolated dune, so there weren't many distractions for a change. I rested my head on her belly and listened to the rhythm of the sea. I felt the rising and falling of Laura's breathing and the slow thud of my own pulse.

Back home, I went over my check list and made sure that everything was in order. I would drive out to Lloyd Harbor, as though I was reporting for work. I would shoot her at some point and bury her in the woods, where it is not likely that she will be discovered before we leave for Bermuda. I will come back to Garden City, change back to Marc, pick up my own car and appear at Laura's as though I had just arrived from New York.

I committed all the details to memory and repeated them over and over again to myself until they threatened to lose their meaning.

I took a bath, allowing the water to get as hot as my skin could stand. Clouds of steam rose around me. Water beaded on the mirror and streaked down. It was difficult to breathe and I felt myself sweating. I did not turn off the hot water until it was actually painful. I enjoyed the pain. I enjoyed the heat and the sweat. It calmed me down. I almost forgot what I was about to do. My eyelids were heavy. I wanted to sleep. I wanted to disappear into the mist.

After a while, I got out and dried myself. I wrapped a towel around my middle and had a drink in the coolness of the living room. I went to the window, where the blind was open, and looked across the way for my Lady of the Geraniums. I had not seen her lately and expected her window to be dark. But it wasn't. Her blind, too, was open, and she, too, was standing there looking across the darkness. She had nothing on and she was holding a glass. My heart jumped and a hum of excitement and fear went through my body. I had an impulse to hide, not because I was embarrassed, but because I didn't want to frighten her away. But I did not move. Something in her posture and whole appearance assured me that things would be different this time.

I undid the towel and let it fall. She was looking directly at me. She tilted her head and raised her glass in a toast as if to salute me. Automatically, I too lifted my glass, and we both drank. Then she smiled or perhaps she laughed. I trembled with excitement and felt myself tumbling down a long hill. I couldn't stop. She was watching and laughing. Her mouth was open, her head moved from side to side. I was glad I could not hear her voice. As I plunged into the abyss, I saw her hand move towards the blind. She paused for a long moment, her laughter undiminished, and then, as though she were operating a guillotine, she let the executioner's arm fall, cutting off everything—light, flesh, laughter, life!

It is late now and I am unable to sleep. I am like a child on Christmas Eve. Only this time I am the bearer of gifts, the Santa Claus of Death. Tomorrow everything will be different. I will be free—out of the old bind. Out of the old life.

174

Sunday, 1 June

It's all over now. I came out this morning in my rented car, a bearded middle-aged Englishman in search of a new life, a kind of artist, a man of understanding but a man destined for oblivion the moment his mission in life was completed. My suitcase was empty. A dead man doesn't need clothes. In my pocket, was the gun. I kept reminding myself that everything would be all right as long as I didn't have to touch her. That was the important thing.

I went up the driveway, past the big house and on to the caretaker's cottage. It was a lovely morning. The woods beyond the cottage were alive with birds. The air was cool and clear. The world in its early summer loveliness was like a pubescent girl. The interior of the cottage was a Vermeer painting, with sunlight slanting through the door and window to give all colour and form a thrilling clarity and definition. And there on the dropleaf table in the small living room was a sparkling white vase, exploding with peonies. I walked through every room, touching the dustless furniture, imagining it all as mine.

When I appeared at the house, I found Gertrude on the patio, beyond the grape arbour and the little fountain for the birds. She was seated at a wrought iron table, holding a delicate blue coffee cup to her lips. Opposite her another place was set, presumably for me.

Since our last meeting, the level of our intimacy had somehow increased. We spoke as old friends or lovers might about ourselves and each other. But I did not forget this time what I had to do. After a while, we carried our coffee cups into the kitchen and put them on the counter beside the sink. I followed her around as she chatted on about a list for the hardware store. And then, suddenly, I knew the moment had arrived. After ages of erosion I felt a giant piece of land slip away inside of me. My hand was actually on the cold handle of the revolver. I tightened my grip and began to remove it slowly from my pocket.

Suddenly the phone rang. We were standing in the living room beside the French doors. The universe stalled.

I held my breath while Gertrude answered. Her eyes were on me. She made it perfectly clear to me that she was speaking to Laura. 'No, Marc is not here,' she said. And then she said it again and again, each time a little louder, each time staring at me harder, until she put down the phone and moved towards me across the oriental rug.

In the next moment, when I finally allowed myself to breathe again, I felt all the tension slip away and a great lightness came over me. *Marc is not here,* I repeated to myself. *Marc is not here.* It's that simple. Marc has disappeared. There is no longer any problem. A tiny item in the *Times*, as tiny perhaps as Gertrude's ad for a caretaker, a brief investigation, and then oblivion —not even a body to discover floating face downwards in the river.

Gertrude was beside me. She was saying something about her son and his fiancée and she was smiling. I felt her hand slip into mine and we walked out through the French doors into the sunlight.